*it,
ng
of
ss*

*ie.
ke
rs*

What's not to love. There's magic, romance, friendship, an evil coven on their backs. This is a great start in what's measuring up to be a thrill ride of a series, and I'll be re-reading the first until the next is released because I just can't get over how enticing the story is."
—*EmbraceYouMag.com*

The Coven Series

By Trish Milburn

Book One: WHITE WITCH

Book Two: BANE

Book Three: MAGICK (coming 9/2012)

Bane

Book Two of the COVEN series

by

Trish Milburn

Bell Bridge Books

Bell Bridge Books
PO BOX 300921
Memphis, TN 38130
Print ISBN: 978-1-61194-134-0

Bell Bridge Books is an Imprint of BelleBooks, Inc.

We at BelleBooks enjoy hearing from readers.
Visit our websites – www.BelleBooks.com and
www.BellBridgeBooks.com.

10 9 8 7 6 5 4 3 2 1

Cover design: Debra Dixon
Interior design: Hank Smith
Photo credits:
Cover Art © Christine Griffin

:Lbe:01:

Dedication

To Shane—Every girl deserves a hero, and you're mine.

Acknowledgements

Thanks to Joss Whedon and Eric Kripke, whose work inspired me to create the Coven series at a point when I needed a story about which to get excited.

Chapter One

I close the thick history of Salem, Massachusetts, and grip the sides tightly, as if the force might miraculously make the book useful to me. It doesn't work. The dusty old book reveals nothing about the world's dark witch covens or how I can defeat them. Not even a hint of a mention. Just like all the other books I've looked at over the past two hours.

A growl of frustration wells within me, but I keep it contained. The last thing I want from the other patrons of the Salem Public Library is undue attention. More than ever, keeping a low profile is imperative. I can't have the covens figuring out where I am before I know how to at the very least neutralize them, before I confirm I really am a white witch and what exactly that means.

I look at my fingertips. Smooth, unmarred skin stares back at me. You'd never know that only days ago I had massive amounts of lightning-like power shooting out of those same fingertips, sending the unsuspecting members of my coven fleeing. I can still feel the thrum of power coursing through my body like it had when I was standing on that mountain in North Carolina, funneling magic up from the earth, through my body, and letting it explode into the night. It had frightened me as much as it had my father and other relatives, maybe more. That's why I have to know what it means, how to control it, if it's a good or bad thing.

I stand and return the book to the shelf where I found it. When I step between the stacks, I do growl. Well, actually it's my stomach reminding me that I haven't eaten in something like fifteen hours. As I stare at the shelves of books in front of me, I can't face delving into yet another one right now, not on an empty stomach.

I take a moment to rub my tired, burning eyes before I climb the stairs to the second floor to find Egan Byrne, the only other witch in the world I trust.

"Find anything?" I ask when I find Egan tucked away in a corner working on his laptop.

He leans back and stretches. "Nothing we didn't already know." He turns sideways in the chair and stares at me. "Why am I looking at public records? You know I'm not going to find anything useful."

"You don't know that. I refuse to believe there isn't the least speck of information that will point us toward . . . something that will help us. Some mention of our families, lore about white witches, details about the formation of the covens, even something that's framed as fiction that might in fact be truth."

"What if there are no answers for what happened at Shiprock? What do we do then?"

I think back to the spirit coven that had inhabited the Shiprock outcropping on the side of the mountain above Baker Gap, how many people they'd killed over the centuries, how I'd destroyed them. How I'd then managed to turn myself into a type of magical conduit, lighting up the dark night like the sun.

"There *are* answers," I say. "We just have to find them." I have to believe that.

Movement catches my eye, and I look past Egan to see a librarian looking our direction. When we make eye contact, she smiles. I offer what I hope looks like an easy smile back, then refocus my attention on Egan. When he looks like he might ask another question, I hold up my hand to stop him.

"Not here. Let's get some lunch. My stomach is about to consume itself."

"That's the best idea you've had all day," he says and quickly shuts down his computer and slips it into his backpack.

Egan tries to hide it, but I notice him wincing as we descend the stairs. We're a block up the street, heading toward downtown, before I mention it. "How are you feeling?"

"Fine."

"You don't have to be all macho about it. You were seriously injured, Egan. You could have died."

"But I didn't." I can tell by the way he says it that he doesn't want to think about the injuries he sustained during the battle with my coven. Or how he'd walked out of that hospital, leaving the only girl he'd ever truly cared about behind without even a goodbye.

A lump forms in my throat. I know how he feels because he wasn't the only person to leave someone he loved back in Baker Gap. I'm lucky if I can go five minutes without thinking about Keller. My greater-good reason for being in Salem might be to find a way to make sure the dark covens of the world can no longer hurt anyone, witch or non-witch. But I have a much more personal reason for wanting to be free to live how and where I want. I want more than anything to be with Keller as I was during my brief time living my dream of being a normal girl. Or as normal as a witch dating a supernatural hunter could get anyway. I want to be able to hang out and do goofy things with my best friend Toni, who happens to be Keller's cousin and the girl for whom Egan fell hard.

We slip into a sandwich shop at the edge of downtown and place our orders. After we pick up our sandwiches and fill our drink cups, we retreat to the far back corner of the dining area, as far away from the other customers as possible.

Egan is evidently as hungry as I am because he dives into his sandwich like he hasn't eaten since he left Texas weeks ago. While we're stuffing our faces, a young woman on her cell phone slips into a chair at the table next to us. Irritation has me staring a hole through her. I'm surprised she can't feel the burning of my gaze, but she's too wrapped up in her conversation to notice.

I shake my head and shift my eyes away from her, already planning to get a good night's sleep later so I'm not so grumpy. I notice Egan giving me an odd look, like he can read my mind. That gives me a jolt and makes me focus on what I'd thought had been my imagination. As I'm trying to figure out a way to ask the questions pressing against the edges of my brain, the chatty woman jumps up from the table and heads toward the front of the restaurant. I look over my shoulder in time to see her hug another woman, and both of them head for a table near the front window.

I turn back to Egan before someone else decides to park next to us. "Did anything change for you that night at Shiprock?" I ask.

"What do you mean?"

I hesitate and look down at my hands wrapped around my turkey club, suddenly worried that he might think I'm crazy, that all that power damaged me somehow. Though I didn't invite him to join up with me in hiding, I don't think I can face doing this alone again. He's the only friend I have left.

"Jax, what is it?"

I meet his eyes. "I feel like I've changed since that night, like my senses are heightened."

"Like you're not just aware of my energy signature anymore, and you can sense my feelings?"

My mouth opens in surprise. "I thought I was imagining it. So you can sense my feelings, too?"

Egan nods. "I don't know if it's just another thing that the covens didn't tell us about, or if it has something to do with your little glow show during the fight, but something just sort of popped open inside me."

I consider Egan's revelation for a few seconds. "Not like mind reading. Just our previous sensory abilities, only heightened."

"Yeah."

I drop my sandwich into the little plastic basket it came in and sit back in my chair. "Instead of answers, I feel like all I find are more questions." Like if this ability has changed in us because of what happened during the battle, what else might have changed?

"Does feel like we're stumbling around in the dark, not even realizing the thing we're looking for is a light switch."

I pop a potato chip in my mouth as I try to sort out my thoughts. When I swallow it, I lean forward. "I feel like if we can get to the source, something, anything about the formation of the covens, we can pull that thread and see where it leads."

"You don't believe what we've been told about the covens' beginnings?"

"After finding out we were lied to about having our full powers before we turn seventeen, I'm looking at everything the covens ever told us as suspect."

"And what they didn't tell us." He looks past me to make sure no one is nearby. "Like do white witches really exist, and what they can do."

"Yeah. I'd kind of like to know if I'm some sort of freak of witch nature."

"And if it can help us."

I nod. "If there is any information on defeating the dark covens, it has to be here where it all began. It's the only thing that makes sense to me."

"Even though I found the Beginning Book in Texas a Frisbee throw from the Mexican border?"

"Minus the one page that may have the information we need." Long thought lost or destroyed or perhaps even a myth, the Beginning Book was supposedly forged at the same time as the covens, created by the same dark magic drawn from the earth in Salem. Egan had found it, but one page was suspiciously missing, torn out for some reason I feel in my gut is important. "We have to have a starting place, and to me Salem is the most logical."

"And you think you're going to find your answers at the public library?"

"Maybe, maybe not. But hopefully I'll find something that will at least point us in the right direction. There has to be a way to defeat them for good, and I intend to find it. I don't want to spend the rest of my life on the run. I want to go back to Baker Gap."

Egan doesn't respond, and I don't press him to, especially since we get new neighbors, an older couple who might have to be rushed to the ER with chest pain if they knew they were sitting next to real witches with very real powers. I sense the older man staring at me, but I ignore him. I hate that my looks draw so much unwanted attention, but I'm used to it. And it's definitely not at the top of my main concerns list.

We slip into silence and eat our meals. When I finish, I grab my thick jacket from the back of my chair. "I'm going back to the library, take a crack at the area's genealogy records."

I make the mistake of meeting his gaze, seeing his doubt that I'll find anything useful. But I have to try. My gut is telling me that if I just look long enough, dig deep enough, that I'll find a clue that will lead to another and so on.

"I'll catch up with you later," he says. "I'm going to do some Internet research." By Internet research, I know he means hacking his normal information sources to see if anyone has figured out where we are yet.

When I head out the door, the wind whips around the corner of the building, smacking me with cold. We're still more than a month from the start of winter, but already it feels like the inside of a freezer to me. Granted, I've lived most of my life in balmy Miami, at least until a couple of months ago when I took the drastic step of fleeing my coven. I know it will be the end of me if they ever find me again and I can't pull out another miracle, but I long ago accepted that as a possible outcome if the other choice was living within the confines of the coven for the rest of my days. I don't have it in me to kill without remorse, to take from others on a whim. That makes me a threat to the coven way of life, expendable like my mother was.

A flicker of awareness causes my power to stir. Unwilling to make a sudden move and give myself away, I instead slow then stop and pretend to read a historical marker. Casually, I look back over my shoulder but don't see anything out of the ordinary. I begin walking slowly then stop at a crosswalk to allow the traffic to pass. I open my senses up a tad more but don't detect any witch power signatures. But there is . . . something. What is it? As I try to wrap my senses around it, the disturbance disappears.

I scan my surroundings as I cross the street, wondering why I sensed something not quite right. By the time I reach the library, I still haven't found an answer, and I don't like not knowing. I glance back down the street one more time, but all I see is the librarian from earlier getting out of her car, probably coming back from her lunch break. She smiles again as she notices me.

"Back for more reading?" she asks as she approaches while smoothing the sides of her hair that's pulled back in a cute chignon.

"Yeah."

"You seemed very into what you were reading earlier."

I fall into step with her as we climb the steps up to the brick and brownstone building that was once the home of some wealthy merchant. "Yeah, I tend to get lost in books."

That much is true. Of course I don't have to tell her that I've often buried myself in books to avoid the reality of life within a dark witch coven.

"Well, if you need anything, just let me know."

"Okay, thanks." I wish I could enlist her help, but I can't exactly ask the local librarian if she knows how to rid the world of dark witch covens, can I? But suddenly the needle-in-a-haystack nature of my search for answers hits me. I shake it off as we cross the threshold. It's too soon to be discouraged. I've barely scratched the surface of what the library has to offer. With that in mind, I head for the Salem History Room on the second floor.

Several people are busy searching the Internet on the Reference Room's computers. Most of them don't pay me any attention, for which I'm thankful. But before I can sigh with relief, one guy glances up and gets that dazed look I so hate. Before he can say anything, I open the glass door etched with a sailing ship and slip inside the history room. Fate must be otherwise occupied today because the guy thankfully doesn't follow me.

I close the door behind me then scan the offerings—birth and death records, city statistics, newspaper clippings, annual addresses of the mayor. My gaze lights on the section devoted entirely to the Salem witch trials, and a sense of dread and foreboding shifts within me. Sixteen months of hysteria that led to three centuries of retribution by the dark covens I aim to destroy. I glance toward the door and take a deep breath.

There's a part of me that whispers that it's no more than wishful thinking to expect that I'll find anything here that will tell me if I'm indeed a white witch, if that was how I was able to win the battle I should have lost. That doubt tells me that if the covens have a vulnerability, I won't find it here where mere mortals could stumble across it. Still, what choice do I have? I have to start somewhere. I'm certainly not going to find a way to live free from fear by moving from one town to the next in an effort to stay one step ahead of my coven. That's no sort of life.

I step forward and run my fingers over the spines of the books, wishing my power would somehow let me know which volume, if any, holds clues. Why can't I be more like Buffy the Vampire Slayer and have a brainy Giles to go to for help?

I pull a book about the families involved in the witch trials from the shelf and grab a collection of old maps on my way to the table in the center of the room. I lose track of time as I go back and forth from reading the book to examining the maps of 17th century land holdings.

My heart speeds up when I see my last name, but then I realize the correct combination of letters doesn't spell Pherson but rather MacPherson. Still, I make note of where I find it in case it's a connection to my ancestors. Had our family changed our name in the intervening years? Lots of families did that to escape persecution of one type or another.

When the door starts to open, I stiffen. But it's only the friendly librarian again.

"Is there anything I can help you with?" Am I imagining a hint of too much curiosity in her eyes? Or is it just a librarian's natural need to know more?

"No, I'm fine. Thank you."

"Okay, but if you change your mind, this is my area of expertise," she says as she taps the cover of one of the books about the Salem witch trials.

My mouth opens a little, wanting to ask the dozens of questions that come flooding into my mind. But I only nod, not sure if this turn of events is lucky for me or something I should be concerned about.

She crosses to the shelf on the back wall and retrieves a thin volume. She returns to the table where I'm sitting and places the book next to the ones already there. "This is one of the better ones, in my opinion."

I glance at the title. *The Salem Witch Trials, a Concise History.* "Thanks." I glance past her toward the shelf. "There certainly are a lot of them."

"People are fascinated by the dark periods of history. The Plague, the Holocaust." She motions toward the shelf behind her. "The infamous Salem witch trials."

She retrieves a book someone has left unshelved and puts it back in its proper place. "Are you visiting Salem? I haven't seen you here before yesterday."

A frisson of unease makes me want to squirm, but she's really given me no reason to think she's anything other than a friendly, eager bookworm. Still, I have to be careful until I know more about my situation and what it means for not only my future but also Egan's.

"Yes."

The woman keeps watching me as if she expects more. When I give her nothing else, the librarian smiles and glances at the clock. "Okay. We close this level fifteen minutes before the library, so you've got five more minutes."

I glance at the clock and see that I've read the afternoon away. I nod then deliberately lower my attention to the book in front of me.

"Well, if you come back and decide you need help finding anything, just let me know. My name's Sarah."

"Okay," I respond without looking up. I hope she attributes this to my desire to make the most of my research time and not rudeness or anything suspicious.

When Sarah closes the glass door behind her, I stare after her. I don't sense anything supernatural about her, so at least she's not a coven witch.

I return my attention to the materials spread out in front of me and feel suddenly overwhelmed, as if I've only taken a tiny bite out of an enormous pie. How in the world am I going to get through all this information without help?

I press the base of my palm against my forehead to stave off an encroaching headache that feels like someone has started a jackhammer against the inside of my skull. I have to find some balance between wanting all the information right now and the reality of what I can do on my own.

I glance toward the closed door, thinking about Sarah's offer to assist me. Is there a way I can take her up on her offer without telling her the whole truth? I take a deep breath and tell myself I'll think about it more after I get some rest. Since I can't check out any of the special collections, I use my new phone to take pictures of several pages of the book and a couple of the old speeches by former mayors. In response, the jackhammer gets turned up a notch, and I grind my teeth to keep from screaming at the tiny jackhammer operator. Yeah, that wouldn't make me look crazy at all.

As I stare at the piles of research and think of the hours it's going to take to sift through it, I realize that maybe I am crazy.

Sarah and her fellow librarian are otherwise occupied when I head downstairs five minutes before closing time. I slip past the circulation desk and out into the night to find Egan waiting for me.

"What are you doing here?" I ask as I descend the steps to the sidewalk.

"I'm starving. Thought you might be hungry, too. And no offense, but you can't cook. I've never known anyone who could ruin ramen noodles."

I shrug. "It's a talent."

He snorts then nods toward the Jeep behind him.

"Do I even want to know where that came from?" I ask.

"Nope."

"We said no powers, Egan, not unless absolutely necessary." Like when we'd used the tiniest sliver of our power of manipulation to maneuver our way into a rental cottage this morning. After several days of lying low after leaving Baker Gap and sleeping in my Volkswagen Beetle, we'd needed actual beds and to hide the Beetle and Egan's Ducati. "We can't afford for the covens to find us before we figure out how to defeat them for good."

"Have a little faith in me, will you? I don't have to use my powers to be persuasive." He gives me a wicked grin, and it makes my heart sink because it's all too familiar. I've seen it at least a dozen times over the years—all before he met and fell for Toni.

"Don't give me that look," he says.

"What look? Oh, you mean the one where I can't believe you've screwed around on Toni after only two weeks."

"Toni's in the past, same as Keller." He pauses, letting his words sink in. "And you're making assumptions. You know what they say about that." Egan climbs into the driver's seat of the Jeep.

I'm tempted to just walk home, but it's flipping cold. I can't imagine what full-on winter is going to feel like. Of course, I might be nowhere near Salem then.

I slide into the Jeep and shut the door harder than necessary.

"You don't have the right to be mad at me. It was your idea to leave," Egan says.

"You agreed."

"I did, and I'm moving on. You should, too."

I stare at him. "How do you do that, just turn off emotions?"

I expect him to give some flippant answer, but instead he stares out the windshield. "Lots of practice."

So he isn't over Toni, no matter how much he might act otherwise.

"I'm not so sure that's a good thing, considering who we are."

He looks at me then. "There's a difference between turning off what has to be turned off and giving in to our darker natures."

I don't respond, instead looking back at the thus-far useless library.

"No luck?" he asks.

"Not yet, but I'm not giving up."

"We can do the impossible, and it'll make us mighty?"

I shift my gaze to Egan and laugh a little. "You got that from one of Toni's *Firefly* T-shirts."

His eyes dim, and my new sensory abilities tell me he is hurting the same as I am. But before I can pull a girl move and ask him about his feelings, he turns the ignition key.

"Where to?" he asks.

"Wherever. I'm not all that hungry."

"You better fuel up because we're going to have a long night," he says.

"You got something planned I don't know about?"

He nods toward the library. "I figure it's time I fall on my sword and drag my ass back here. We'll get a lot more research done if we both go at it without interruptions."

"You know they're closed, right?"

He smiles that wicked grin of his. "And I know the security in some rinky-dink library is no match for me."

I shake my head. "Okay then, I'm going to need some industrial strength coffee if I'm going to stay up all night. And an ibuprofen the size of a grapefruit."

"I have the perfect place." Egan puts the Jeep in gear and drives away from the curb.

As we stop at the end of the street, I look over to find Sarah the librarian standing next to her car in the parking lot. Despite the dimness of the light out there, I get the weirdest feeling that she's watching us. And that she knows exactly what we're up to.

In that moment, I wonder if our new sensory abilities extend to regular humans. Or if Sarah is much more than a helpful librarian.

Chapter Two

Thanks to Egan's breaking-and-entering abilities, we are able to examine the majority of the books and documents in the Salem History Room in three nights. What little is left, I plan to get through today. I try not to feel discouraged that so far nothing has given me anything approaching the answers I need.

Egan's mood isn't faring any better. This newfound ability to sense each other's feelings isn't really a blessing. I don't know if his sour mood is because of our lack of progress or him missing Toni, but I can't take much more of it. I've already nearly bitten his head off half a dozen times. So I send him off to play tourist at the various witch-related sites around town to see if any of them hold anything more than hokey dramatizations of the infamous Salem witch trials.

When I enter the library, I don't see Sarah. The librarian isn't on the second level either. Finally, something is going my way.

Of course, that thought jinxes everything. When I open the door to the Salem History Room, someone is already seated at the table, a guy about my age. By the time I see him, it will draw more attention to me if I turn around and leave. So I make my way toward the drawers of maps.

"Hey," the guy says.

"Hey."

"Figured I'd be the only teenager spending my Saturday afternoon in here," he says.

I turn toward the table with a stack of old property maps. "Guess not." *Come on, dude, take a hint. Short answers mean I don't want to talk.*

He taps the book in front of him. "History homework. You?"

"No, I've graduated." It's the first time I've had to use the story Egan and I concocted on the way to Salem, that we're brother and sister and already eighteen. We can't risk compelling someone to help us enroll in school, so we have to rely on our fake IDs to keep away the questions about why we aren't living with adults.

"Just a history lover then?"

Chatty, isn't he? I meet his gaze for the first time and realize not only is he good-looking with sandy brown hair and hazel eyes, but he doesn't have that stunned look on his face that most guys get around me. I don't know whether to be wary or thankful.

"Yeah. Doing a bit of genealogy." I'm not sure why I added that last bit, but it's out there now, and I have to go with it.

"Your family's from here?"

I nod.

"Maybe I could help. I've lived here my whole life. I'm Rule, by the way. Rule Latimer."

Odd name. I nearly laugh at the irony of a girl named Jaxina thinking anyone's name is unusual.

"That's okay. Don't want to keep you from your homework."

"It's no problem." He knocks his knuckle against the book in front of him. "I've got plenty of time to work on this."

He seems so open, so willing to help that I find myself smiling. At the same time, I let a minuscule fraction of my power reach forth to examine him. When I detect no power signature, I make an executive decision. After all, I've been able to ask Sarah a question here and there without revealing too much of the truth. Maybe this Rule Latimer will prove useful.

"I think my family lived in this area ages ago, maybe in some of the earliest settlements."

"What's the family name?"

I don't immediately answer, wondering if I am about to make a huge mistake. But what I've done so far has yielded next to nothing of use. Maybe it's time for a leap of faith. And if it is a mistake, I'll deal with it then.

"Pherson."

Rule doesn't respond. Instead, he stares at me long enough to make my senses twitch. But then he scrunches his forehead for a moment before standing and crossing to the shelf next to the map cabinet. He scans the spines of several large books, and I get the distinct feeling the gears in his head are turning faster than normal. He seems to find what he's looking for and pulls a book from the shelf. He places an old, fragile-looking text on the table in front of me.

"These are some of the oldest land records for this part of Massachusetts." He opens the book to the index and starts running his finger down a list of names written in that old-timey, flowing script that's hard to read.

I don't move, don't even dare to breathe too much. Rule stands close enough that I feel the warmth from his body and smell the scent of some sort of woodsy soap. It would be an intoxicating combination were I not in love with someone else. Even so, I can appreciate his attractiveness and wonder if I read too much into his initial reaction to my surname.

"I'm not seeing any Phersons." Why doesn't he sound surprised? Is it just because he's never heard it before, or because he has? He straightens, giving me room to breathe. I glance up at him, trying to read his expression. While he wears a friendly smile, it seems . . . more reserved.

I shrug. "Oh, well. Guess they must have been from somewhere else. Thanks for looking." I'm not giving up, just not involving this boy, this stranger any more than I already have. No matter how cute he is.

He seems to shake off whatever was bothering him and smiles, and I find myself liking him on no more than instinct. I just hope my instincts haven't been compromised by drawing in all that dark energy at Shiprock. I hate that I don't know the extent of the effects on me. I feel different, but I can't totally put my finger on it. Sort of tense.

"No problem. Happy to help." He shifts to return the book to its spot on the shelf.

As he stretches his arms above his head, I notice just how

tall and lanky he is. When I see how well his jeans fit, I jerk my gaze away and hate myself. How can I even notice another guy, especially when I scolded Egan for moving on from Toni so easily? Maybe my attraction to him is what's making me tense, because in my heart it feels wrong.

Needing some fresh air and a lot of distance from Rule, I stand.

"You're leaving?" he asks.

I don't look at him. "Yeah. Just remembered I've got to be somewhere in a few minutes." That excuse probably sounds as lame as it feels coming off my tongue, but it doesn't matter. Something about Rule is putting me on edge, and the last thing I need is one more reason to feel fidgety.

"Okay. See you around," he says.

"Yeah, maybe." I quickly return the materials I pulled. I don't exactly run out the door, but Rule would have to be oblivious to not notice how quickly I make a getaway.

Halfway back to the cottage, my phone rings.

"Tell me you've got something," I say when I answer Egan's call.

"Sorry to disappoint. I'm beginning to think this town has never seen a real witch."

"I know the feeling. I don't think there's any doubt about the covens doing one heck of a cover-up."

"Why do you think they did it? I mean, if they were suddenly more powerful than everyone else, why hide it?"

I think for a moment about all the coven members I know, their personalities, their tendencies. "Maybe it started out as protection or even some leftover fear from the trials. But now, I just think they get a kick out of it, watching the non-witches go about their days totally in the dark."

"Hard to believe no one has let it slip in three hundred years," Egan says.

"You know what happens if someone makes a wrong step and goes against the covens."

We both knew it all too well.

"Do you think we're even looking in the right place? What

if every single thing we've been told is a lie, and we're on a wild goose chase?"

I shake my head at that possibility, refusing to believe it. "They've lied, yes, but if there's one thing I think the covens told the truth about, it's that they began in Salem."

"Then they've been damn good at covering their tracks."

"We just have to dig deeper. Maybe we're looking in the wrong places, the obvious places. It would make sense that if there's information to be had here, it's shoved away somewhere we'd never think to look."

Egan makes a sound of frustration. "Pick up a six-pack of Dr. Pepper on the way back."

"What am I, your errand girl?"

"You owe me after all the garbage I forced myself through today. Seriously, some of these displays haven't been changed since Kennedy was president. And the hyperbole is crazy. One dude wrote about how the witch trials were God's way of cutting out the black heart of Satan. I bet he was a barrel of laughs at parties."

"Pretty sure they thought parties were of Satan, too."

My stomach churns at the thought that despite my desire to be different, I am still a product of the dark covens. It's in the blood, and that's one thing about myself I can't change. Does that make me a part of the black heart of Satan? Even if I am a white witch, can I ever really leave all my darkness behind?

After I end the call, a prickle of awareness skitters along my skin, that same feeling of being watched again but slightly different. This time I stop and turn quickly, hoping to get a glimpse of whoever is there. But when I search the shadows next to the buildings lining the street, I don't see anyone. I risk letting go of the tight rein I have on my power and let it sizzle at my fingertips as I retrace my steps and use my senses to search for another witch.

After five minutes of checking doorways and alleys, I come up empty. But just as I turn to head back home, convinced I've imagined it again, I catch a scent that seems out of place. I slowly inhale to take in the woodsy scent fully. I'm not sure why, but my heart sinks when I confirm it isn't coming from any of the trees lining the street. Instead, it smells exactly like Rule's masculine soap.

He isn't a witch, of that I'm sure. I sense none of the darkness inherent in witches, no discernible energy signature. So why is he so interested in me, especially when he didn't act like most guys do around me? I was thankful for his lack of reaction at first, but now I wonder if his not being mesmerized by me is a confirmation that something is actually off about him. The same something that had made him hesitate and pull back at the library.

Only one way to find out. I let my sense of smell lead me down the alley to the next street over. As I exit the alley onto Front Street, the scent angles to the left and across, straight into a shop. The oval sign hanging over the front door says Wiccan Good Herbs. I edge into the darker shadows next to the buildings on my side of the street. From that vantage point, I watch as Rule walks behind the counter and gives an older woman a kiss on the cheek.

I close my eyes and search the building with my senses. There's a slight vibration I can't identify, and I don't like not knowing. I fight the sudden urge to storm inside and seek out the source, to demand to know why Rule was following me. I'm sick and tired of questions and burn with the need for answers. I manage to keep myself from following through on the urge. Barreling headlong into the unknown doesn't seem like the best tactic if I want to stay under the coven radar, if I want to stay alive.

I want to believe this is nothing more than a boy being attracted to me, but my instincts are insisting there is something else going on. And my instincts are rarely wrong.

"Tell me again why you're dragging me to an herb shop," Egan says as he parks the Jeep half a block down from Wiccan Good Herbs. "Haven't I done enough with my fabulous computer mojo?"

Bane

I give him a squinty-eyed stare. "You're backup. There is something wonky going on here, and I don't want to walk into a trap alone."

"So I get to walk into the trap with you. Some friend you are. I really am of better use alive."

"Maybe we'll find an herb here that can give you some modesty."

"Modesty's overrated."

I roll my eyes and slip out of the Jeep. I'm halfway to the shop before Egan catches up with me.

"You sure you just don't have the hots for this guy?"

I stop and turn toward him. "That might be the stupidest thing you've ever asked me."

He holds up his hands. "Sorry. But you need to let go."

"Like you have?"

"Yeah."

"You forget you can't lie to me anymore," I say. "I can sense when you're not telling the truth."

"Well, that's annoying," he says.

"How about we just both acknowledge that we miss them, and that we're probably going to miss them for a long time?"

Maybe forever.

Egan looks like he's going to respond then stops himself and redirects his gaze down the street. "Fine."

As we enter the shop, my nose twitches with all the fragrances.

"Be with you in a minute," a woman calls out from beyond a curtained doorway.

Egan wanders off to the left, looking as out of place as a dog at a cat convention. He picks up a jar candle.

"Says it is spelled for protection," he says. "Maybe we should get one, or a thousand."

"You don't sound as if you're a believer." An older woman with her hair cut short and wearing long, dangling earrings materializes from behind the curtain. Okay, so she doesn't really materialize, but she does move so softly she barely makes a sound.

I sense a sort of . . . hum about her, and I realize Rule had it, too. I just hadn't been able to put my finger on what was different. I use a touch of my power to dig a little deeper, pulling back layers of energy. This woman's is unfamiliar, not witch, not mortal human. It feels like it might be benign, but it's odd enough to make me wary. She's Wiccan, I presume, but not like any Wiccan I've ever encountered. They've always read like normal humans, but not this woman.

"That a candle in a jar can protect me?" Egan says. "Sorry, but no."

The older woman smiles, and as she moves closer to us, I see that one of her earrings is made up of tiny silver moons, the other of silver suns. "There are a lot of things in this world we don't understand. A little precaution never hurt anyone."

Hmm, that sounded remarkably like what I'd been thinking.

Egan is on the verge of saying something else, but I shoot him a warning look.

"Don't mind my brother," I say. "He's just grumpy because I made him come Christmas shopping with me."

The woman offers a warm smile that for some reason makes me think of spice cookies and hot apple cider. Another layer in what I'm sensing is a very complex person. I wonder what she's hiding, but I know she is hiding something.

"Then I'd best help you find some gifts," the woman says. "What are you looking for?"

I do a quick scan of the shop, looking for Rule and some answers more than anything. But my gaze spots a display of soaps in the corner, and I walk toward it as I keep scanning the interior of the shop. "Maybe some soaps."

"Oh, these are nice, made with goat's milk. Very good for the skin, especially this time of year when everything is so dry."

I only half listen to the woman talk about how the soap is made. The half that isn't listening joins Egan in sensing out the place. There's still that odd little hum in the air, but again, it isn't something I can identify. Maybe all this Wiccan stuff has a hint of power about it, and this woman is just more practiced than the Wiccans I've met before.

"I'll take two of the lavender and one of the cucumber and melon," I say when the woman stops talking. Luckily, both Egan and I stashed away a lot of cash before we fled our covens. At least that's one thing we don't have to worry about.

"Excellent choices," the woman says. She grabs the soaps and heads toward the front counter. "You two just in town visiting? Your accents don't sound local."

"Just moved here," I say, wondering why everyone seems to be asking about where I'm from. Are Salemites just that curious, or am I sending out some sort of "I don't belong here" vibe? I peel back another layer and sense that the woman's question is more than idle curiosity. But why? Is it because of whatever she's hiding? Does she sense I'm a threat to it?

Suddenly, I want nothing more than to know what this woman doesn't want me to know.

"Well, welcome to Salem. I'm Fiona Day." She looks at Egan and I as if expecting a reply.

"Jax, and Mr. Grumpypants is Egan," I say.

"What interesting names."

Before I can focus too much on Fiona's interest in our unusual names, another woman comes through the curtain with a blue-and-white teapot.

"Oh, just in time," Fiona says. "This is my daughter, Adele. She's just made some peppermint tea. You two have some before you go back out into the cold."

"That's okay," I say.

"Oh, I insist. Adele has a knack for making tea."

Not wanting to protest too much, I accept a cup of tea then jerk my head toward the pot so Egan will do the same. I have to bite my tongue to not laugh at the sight of him with a dainty teacup in his hands.

I take a sip and let the warmth and minty flavor flow through me. But just as the tea hits my stomach, I detect something a little off with the flavor. What is that? Maybe a secret ingredient? This is, after all, an herb shop. My natural suspicion flares, but I push it aside. Despite the odd feeling I get around Fiona, she's been nothing but friendly. Just like Rule.

My stomach twists a little, and I wonder if I dismissed my suspicion too quickly.

"Are you okay, dear?" Fiona asks.

I force a smile despite the growing discomfort in my middle. It isn't pain exactly, but it's not pleasant either. More like that queasy feeling you get when you eat something that's a little past its expiration date. Maybe it's nothing more than a mixture that doesn't set well on my stomach. At least I hope that's all it is.

"Yeah. I just think maybe the tea wasn't a good idea on an empty stomach." I glance at Egan and notice he doesn't appear to be on the verge of singing the tea's praises either. In fact, I sense a frisson of his dark power seeping out. I see it in his eyes, feel it in the static in the air.

We have to get out of here before he does something that will bite us in the butt big-time.

I place my tea on the counter, pull out the money for the soaps, and extend it to Fiona.

The older woman stares at me for a moment, as if she's waiting for something to happen, then smiles and accepts the cash. "Thanks for coming in. Hope to see you again soon."

I nod and guide Egan toward the door. When I place my hand on his back, his body is vibrating. That stirs my own power, and not in a good way. A witch's natural instinct when threatened is to lash out, but I remind myself I don't want to be that kind of witch anymore.

We wait until the women inside can no longer see us before either of us speaks.

"What the hell?" Egan says. "I feel like my stomach is tying in knots and I could blast those women into Vermont."

I glance back at the herb shop. "I think something more than peppermint is in that tea."

"But what? And why?"

"I'm not sure we're going to like the answer to either of those questions."

"They're not witches," he says.

"No, but they're not quite human either." If I had doubts before, they're gone. "Maybe the covens have part-supernatural lackeys."

"To do what, poison the tea of any witches who happen to stumble into town?"

"Maybe they're like guard dogs, helping keep the covens secrets hidden away." I point back at the shop. "Because they're hiding something. I felt it."

Egan moans and grabs his stomach. "Well, hopefully they'll still be hiding it tomorrow when I don't feel like my stomach is eating itself."

He seems to be getting the worst end of the tea deal, so I take the car keys and drive us back to the cottage. By the time we get there, I'm feeling better but Egan still looks a bit green. While he goes to the bathroom, I lock the cottage door and scan the night outside. Though I don't sense any witches, real witches anyway, something is definitely tickling my senses. It bothers me that I can't figure out what. That just spurs me to try harder, drawing on a bit more of my magic to feel out the night. But whatever it was is gone now. Nothing out there but dormant vegetation and a slight breeze.

I try not to feel sick as the sound of Egan making himself throw up comes from the bathroom. Thankfully, it doesn't last long and is followed by running water and the sound of him brushing his teeth. When he finally emerges, the green tinge is gone.

"Feel better?" I ask.

"My stomach's not writhing, but I can't say I'm going to be a big fan of tea anytime soon." He gestures toward the window. "See anything?"

I shake my head. "Something weird is going on though."

"Yeah, wouldn't think trying to poison your customers would be good for business." He walks to the sink and fills a glass with water then takes a long drink. "It was a good thing we left when we did. I felt my grip on my power slipping."

"I know. I felt it, too." I pace across the room.

"Maybe they're hunters," Egan says before taking another drink of water.

I shake my head again. "I don't think so. Hunters are more

direct in their methods. Like when Keller's dad shot me, determined to keep my evil presence away from his son."

Part of me wishes Keller were here. I miss his kisses, his arms around me, his knowledge of the supernatural world.

"You know what. I'm tired of dead ends," I say. "I'm ready for some answers."

"You, me and everyone looking for the meaning of the universe."

"Why, or even if, I'm a white witch might not be presenting itself, but I bet we can find out why Fiona and Adele felt it necessary to drug our tea."

Egan leans against the kitchen doorway. "You're just going to march up and ask them?"

"Yeah. I'm in the mood for a direct approach."

Egan smiles. "I like it."

When we reach Wiccan Good Herbs, I use a touch of my power to unlock the front door and stride inside, Egan right behind me. Without pausing, I walk behind the counter and straight into the room behind the curtain.

Adele and Rule jump up from a small, round table covered with herbs and sachets. But Fiona remains seated and doesn't seem the least bit surprised by our entrance.

"I thought you might be back," Fiona says.

"What did you put in our tea?" I ask as I stroll around the edge of the room. I spare Rule a quick glance, and gone is the chipper, friendly appearance he wore at the library.

"Shavegrass," Fiona replies.

"Why?" I ask.

Fiona looks up then and meets my gaze. "We needed to know if you were witches."

I stop and stare at her. "So you know about witches."

"Yes," Fiona says.

Egan approaches the table, his presence large and imposing in the small room. Rule moves to block him from getting too close to Fiona. "You're gonna want to back away, dude," Egan says.

"Not a chance."

Egan gives him a grin that really does look wicked, and I sense the darkness churning inside him.

"Back away, Egan," I say.

He doesn't seem to hear me.

"Now."

I feel him pushing down hard on the dark energy. He slowly backs away from the table, crosses his arms and stares at Rule.

Fiona pats Rule's arm, and his erect posture eases.

"You two are a puzzle," Fiona says. "That you were researching the Pherson family, and the fact that you had a reaction to the shavegrass tells me that you are indeed witches. But you're not flat out writhing in pain as the herb attacks the evil. Have dark witches begun to mix with non-witches? I never thought I'd see the day."

I glance at Egan, thinking of Keller and Toni. When I meet the eyes of first Adele, then Rule and finally Fiona, I know with absolute certainty that these three know about the covens.

"It seems we're both facing some mysteries," I say. "How do you know about real witches?"

"Because we are witches," Fiona replies.

"No, you're not. I'd be able to sense your energy signatures if you were."

"Why do you have those energy signatures?" Fiona asks as she twirls a twig of some herb between her fingers.

"Because we're witches," Egan says, sounding exasperated.

"Because you're post-Salem witch trials witches."

I meet Egan's gaze, and he looks as confused as I am.

"Not every witch family chose to accept the dark power," Rule says. "Some of them fled, hid until the newly formed dark covens left the area."

I stare at Rule, then at the two women. "Your family fled."

"Both the Latimers, Rule's father's line, and the Brandons, my family," Fiona says. "And a few others. The Phersons were not among them."

I look at Rule and realize some of the oddness I'd felt from him at the library was because he wasn't being honest with me. He'd deliberately "helped" me by directing me to documents and books he knew didn't hold any information about my family or the covens.

I shake my head and shift my attention back to Fiona. "I've never heard about any of this."

"Of course, you haven't." Fiona turns in her seat to more fully face me. "I would imagine there are a great many things your family hasn't been honest about."

Though Fiona speaks the truth, I still feel the sting of the words as if I'm being lumped in with the rest of the Phersons. Their blood might run in my veins, but I'm not like them. That night at Shiprock, that bright white light enveloping me proved that. I have to believe that.

"Rule says you were looking for your family line here," Adele says. "Why?"

I look at the woman, who I've figured out is Rule's mother. I consider just how much truth I'm willing to share. After all, I don't know these people or their motivations. But if they have information about the history of the covens I've never heard before, maybe they know how to defeat the covens. And that's information I aim to get. I'll just take it one step at a time and see what I need to reveal in exchange for new information.

"I want to find out if there's a way to neutralize the covens so they can't hurt anyone anymore," I say. "At least not any more than a normal human."

Fiona looks at Egan. "You feel the same way about your coven?"

I find I'm not surprised that Fiona hasn't bought the story that Egan and I are siblings.

Egan hesitates before answering. "Yes."

Fiona exchanges a look with Adele and Rule, then returns her attention to me. "If you're telling the truth, we have similar interests."

"We are," I say.

"How do we know that for sure?" Adele asks, suspicion in her expression.

Annoyance flares within me. Even when I remind myself that she has every reason to be suspicious, my annoyance doesn't dim. "Because if we were like any normal coven witch, you wouldn't be alive right now," I say.

"Because of the tea," Fiona says.

I nod. "Anyone who attacks a coven witch doesn't live long enough to apologize."

"Then why did you come back here?" Adele asks.

"Because we are in Salem seeking information, and I sense that you're hiding something. From us, specifically."

"What type of information?" Fiona asks.

"The kind that keeps the covens out of our lives," Egan says.

"A way to keep them from hurting anyone ever again," I say.

"We don't know how," Adele says.

I look from her to Fiona. "Maybe not, but you're right when you say the covens have lied to us. We need to know the truth."

Fiona holds my gaze for several seconds, assessing, as silence settles around us. "Why you?"

This woman is very good at reading beyond the surface, but I don't detect any malicious intent toward me. "Because I've never known a coven witch to fight the other members of their coven, to defy the darkness, and live to tell the tale. Until I did it."

Fiona's eyes widen slightly, and I sense surprise from Adela and Rule, too.

I decide to dive in, to trust these people I've just met. "Have you ever heard of a white witch?"

I glance at Egan and see the disbelief written plainly across his face.

"No. Why?" Fiona says.

"Because I think I might be one, or at least have the potential to be one."

"Jax," Egan says, warning in his voice.

I wave away his concern. "We don't have all the time in the world," I say, then return my attention to Fiona. "Before we came here, we were in a battle with my coven. It was only the two of us and two of our non-witch friends versus a dozen dark witches. It was at one of the spots where the covens harvested their dark magic. I knew we'd all die if I didn't do something drastic, so I drew more power out of the earth. At first, it was all dark, but then something unexpected happened."

I meet Egan's gaze for a moment before continuing. "I pretty much exploded in light. It totally erased the darkness inside me, and it literally lifted me into the air. Suddenly, I was more powerful than all those coven witches put together. They fled from me."

"That's good, right?" Rule asks.

"It bought us enough time to get away and keep our friends safe. But I'm hesitant to use something I don't understand."

"What have you heard about white witches?" Rule asks.

"Next to nothing," I say. "We always thought what little we heard were just stories told by kids. It wasn't ever something you'd mention to a grown witch."

Fiona takes a deep breath then gives her daughter a meaningful look. Another long moment passes before she stands and walks toward a long worktable along the far wall. She opens a drawer and retrieves something I can't see. When she returns, she extends a crudely made metal cross to me.

"This won't hurt me," I say. "I'm not a vampire. I can go inside a church, touch holy water."

"Then it shouldn't be a problem for you to hold it, should it?"

I take the cross, but instead of it being cool it feels warm in my hand. I turn it over and look at the opposite side, then switch hands. When I glance up at Fiona, she's looking at me as if I'm some sort of complex mathematical equation. "What?"

Instead of answering, she nods toward Egan. "Now you."

With a loud sigh, he takes the cross but immediately tosses it from one hand to the other. "What did you do to make it hot?" He holds it by the tip and twirls it between his fingers.

"Show me your hands," Fiona says as she takes the cross back.

"Why?"

"Just do it," I say, wanting to get past whatever test Fiona is obviously putting us through.

Egan holds up his hands, palms out, and wiggles his fingers. Then he points at the cross. "This proves nothing. Any dark coven witch could come in here and hold that."

"No, they couldn't," Fiona says. "That's not just any cross. It's made from two of the iron nails that were used to nail Christ to the cross."

Egan snorts.

"What, is that more unbelievable than the existence of dark witches with incredible powers?" Fiona asks.

"How do you know it's real?" I ask. "What is it supposed to do, detect evil?" I think of Keller's bloodstone and how my magic had made it light up like a red Christmas tree bulb.

Fiona holds up the cross. "This was brought to Salem by a minister who witnessed both the witch trials and the formation of the dark covens. He got it from a reliable source in Jerusalem. If a dark witch touches it, its power will melt their skin."

"Sorry, but I think the battery's low," Egan says.

Fiona gives him a look of exasperation, very much like a tired mother whose child challenges her at every turn.

"How do you know it even works?" I ask. "The covens left here after they accepted the dark power and haven't been back. At least that's what we've been told."

"Because the minister saw the power with his own eyes when he pressed it against the forehead of a newly made dark witch," Fiona says.

"Doubtful," I say. "He wouldn't have been allowed to live."

"He was able to flee while the witch tried to recover from the searing pain. And before you ask, I know this to be absolutely true because that minister was my many times great-grandfather."

"Lot of ministers in this evil-fighting business," Egan says under his breath.

I know he's referring to Keller's father, a Methodist minister who takes fighting evil very seriously. I ignore him and stay focused on Fiona. "Maybe the tale got exaggerated over time. It was hot to the touch for Egan, but I only detected a slight warmth."

"Which tells me you two aren't entirely evil." Fiona shakes her head. "I've never heard of such from a witch descended from the families that accepted the dark magic."

"Why did it affect us differently?" Egan asks.

I glance at him and know what he's thinking, that the cross didn't affect me as much because I may be a white witch.

"You're more evil than her," Adele says, matter-of-factly.

Fiona watches me. "Maybe there is something to your white witch theory." Finally, she turns and heads for a cupboard shoved against the back wall.

"Mom," Adele says with a note of warning in her voice.

"They passed the test," Fiona says.

"Not entirely."

"We have waited three centuries for some sign, some way to rid the world of the darkness born in the wake of the trials. There is something different about these two," Fiona says. She stares first at Egan then me. "Something that might finally right wrongs." She turns her attention to her daughter. "Have you ever known my instinct to be wrong about anyone?"

Adele glances at Egan and me before giving what looks like a reluctant shake of her head.

"And it's the first time anything like this has ever happened," Fiona continues. "We've never had this type of power on our side before."

I scrunch my forehead. "Your side?"

"We have a lot to discuss," Fiona says. When she opens the cupboard, there are no shelves holding supplies as I expect. The older woman gestures toward the yawning darkness at the top of a set of descending stairs. "You ready for some answers?"

I stand still as possibilities run through my head. Is this a trap? What's at the bottom of those stairs? But I think about how Egan and I have been flying blind lately and how the covens are no doubt looking for a way to defeat us once and for all.

I glance at Adele and don't sense duplicity. When I meet

Rule's gaze, I hold it. To his credit, he doesn't lower his or look away. For a moment, he reminds me a bit of Keller, not in looks but in an inherent rightness. That's what tips my decision.

I take the first step toward the stairs.

Chapter Three

The scents of cool earth and old paper assault me as I descend the stone steps. Ahead of me, Fiona flips a light switch, and a basement stretches out in front of us. Floor-to-ceiling bookshelves line every stone wall but one. Instead, it's covered with what look like maps. A wooden table with eight chairs sits in the middle of the room.

"What is all this?" I ask.

"Everything my family has ever collected over the years since the Salem witch trials on the existence of witches," Fiona says.

When I reach the bottom of the stairs, I slowly round the room looking at the spines of old books and pieces of yellowed paper stacked on the shelves beside the books. When I reach the maps, I realize they look a lot like the property maps I examined at the library. Only these are slightly different.

My breath catches in my throat when I notice my last name. I touch it with my finger, not sure it's real.

"That was a prime piece of land," Rule says as he walks up beside me. "Good soil, next to a creek." He lifts his finger and traces it along the edge of the property. "This line of trees is still there."

I notice that Rule has nice fingers. Long, straight, strong. I mentally shake myself and bring Keller's face to mind. Thinking of him is always accompanied by a pang of longing. A longing I have to forget in order to focus on the task at hand.

"Are you okay?"

At Rule's question, I shove away thoughts of the boy I left behind along with a large piece of my heart and refocus on the one who might be able to give me some answers.

"Yeah." I spare him only a glance, but even that feels

wrong. Needing some distance from him, I walk toward one of the bookshelves and scan the spines. Some are so old that the titles are either faded almost beyond recognition or not visible at all.

"Why do you have all this stuff hidden down here?" Egan asks as he paces along the opposite wall's collection of reading material.

"Our family knew that what had really happened here in Salem on the heels of the witch trials would be lost to history if someone didn't bear witness," Fiona says. "But they also knew that they couldn't get caught, that they'd lose their lives just the same as those poor innocent souls did. Only this time they'd be murdered to ensure their silence, by people who'd once been just like them."

"What did your family think would come from writing everything down?" Egan asks.

"Maybe it was as simple as making sure the truth wasn't erased." Fiona runs her hand along the frayed cover of a book on the table. "Or maybe they hoped that someday the information would be useful in changing things."

"Getting rid of the covens, you mean?" I ask.

Fiona meets my eyes. "Perhaps."

I let my gaze wander around the room. "You'd think if there were answers here, someone would have found them already."

"Or maybe we just didn't know what to look for," Rule says as he steps up beside his grandmother. "After all, none of us knows what it's like to live inside one of the dark covens."

"Count yourself lucky," I say.

"We do, every day," Adele says. Of the three family members, Adele is the one who obviously trusts Egan and me the least. She might prove to be the wisest in the end.

"Maybe we can help each other," Fiona says.

"What makes you think you can trust us?" I ask.

"Intuition. And the fact that you have shown the strength to defy your covens. We have never been able to do more than keep a record of history because we have no real powers, not like you two."

"But we're the kind of witches your family fled rather than be like."

Fiona fixes her gaze on me, seeming to look deeper than any human truly can. "No, I don't believe you are. Otherwise you wouldn't be here." She gestures toward the contents of the room. "If you were a true dark witch, you would have destroyed all of this on sight then my family and me in the next breath."

"We're not without fault. We've both done things that weren't right."

"Is there anyone alive who can say they've done otherwise?" Fiona asks. She raps her knuckles against the book on the table. "It's too late to dive into this tonight. We've got more than three hundred years worth of history to sift through, but I think bright and early in the morning is soon enough to start."

I almost argue. Every minute counts when I have no doubt the covens are planning their next move. But I keep quiet and resign myself to waiting a few more hours for answers, if they indeed exist.

"What are we looking for anyway?" Adele asks.

"A vulnerability, a chink in the covens' armor," her mother replies. "With Jax and Egan's first-hand knowledge of how the covens operate today, I have no doubt we will find it somewhere in this archive. We've always been operating half-blind, without the knowledge these two bring to the table. We're stronger now."

I hope Fiona is right. But as I look at three centuries of documentation, I can't help but feel like we're facing a search for a needle in a life-or-death haystack.

Egan stops on the path to the cottage a few steps in front of me. Before he has a chance to speak, I sense it, too.

"Someone's been here," I say quietly. I uncurl my fingers and let power spark between my fingertips, ready to fight if necessary. I hope I don't have to, because engaging that much magic will be like sending up a beacon to the covens.

"I'll take the back," Egan whispers.

I nod and wait until he disappears around the corner of the cottage before I approach the front door. When I find the door still locked, I pull the key from my jean pocket and slide it into the lock. I turn the key, open the door and flip on the light switch in one smooth motion. Egan steps through the back doorway at the same moment.

The light illuminates no one other than the two of us, but someone has definitely been in the room during our absence. Everything looks the same as before, but my heightened instincts tell me that in this case looks are definitely deceiving. It's as if the air isn't quite right.

"Not a witch," Egan says.

I'm not so sure. True, there isn't any residual energy signature, but the presence doesn't seem entirely normal either.

"What?" Egan asks.

I notice he is staring at me with his eyebrows drawn together. "Go deeper," I say. "There's something not right. Sort of like Rule and his family, but more."

Egan turns away and reaches out with his senses again. I wait to see if he catches what I did.

"What the hell is that?" he finally says.

I shake my head. "I don't know. But it seems like the closer we get to answers, the more questions we end up having."

"Damn, my head is beginning to hurt." He stalks to the fridge and nabs a cold Dr. Pepper, then downs half of it in one gulp. He scans the room. "Nothing appears to be missing. Of course, they could have been looking for us."

I shake my head. "They'd still be here if that was it." Though I know that the Beginning Book is safe, I pull it from the bag I take everywhere. "You think someone knows we have this?"

Egan shrugs. "I don't think so. I can't imagine how they'd find out. Unless our new *friends* know more than they're saying."

"The bag never left my shoulder," I say. "There's no way they could know."

"Unless it was a plant when I found it in that book shop."

"That seems far-fetched," I say. "Plus the fact that I got a definite vibe that Fiona and her family don't venture from Salem much."

I'm still staring at the plain black cover of the book when I hear footsteps outside. Before I can think about what I'm doing, I'm out the door and shoving the person next to the outside wall of the cottage by the throat. My vision clouds for a moment before I realize Rule's huge eyes are staring back at me. Even when I recognize him, it takes me a couple of seconds to release him.

When I do and take a few steps back, Rule doesn't move. He simply stands still and stares at me, not speaking.

"Sorry," I finally choke out.

"You greet all your visitors like that?" he asks, stepping away from the wall and shaking off what had been a look of terror. In that moment, I know he is well aware of what a coven witch can do to someone without any power.

"No," Egan says. "But then we don't have visitors, unless you count whoever broke into the cottage while we were gone."

Rule rubs his throat as he glances toward the doorway where Egan now stands blocking most of the interior light trying to spill out into the night.

"Anything taken?" Rule asks.

"No, not that we have much anyway," Egan says. "Were you hoping to find something?"

Rule looks genuinely confused. "Me? You know it wasn't me. You were with me."

"But you could be working with someone else," Egan says.

"I'm not." Now it's Rule's turn to sound annoyed. He returns his attention to me.

"Why are you here then?" I ask. "Spying on us to see if we're trustworthy?" I don't seem to be able to curb my sharp tone. Maybe I'm more tired than I realize. I need about twelve hours of solid sleep so I can keep up the fight against the covens all over again tomorrow.

"I don't know about trustworthy, but you certainly have

trust issues."

The darkness inside me makes me want to growl, all out of proportion to the threat Rule poses. Even if he was here for some secret purpose, it's not as if I couldn't squash him as easily as I can a gnat. I close my eyes for a moment and take a deep breath. Maybe if I slept for a month I wouldn't be so edgy. Unfortunately, I don't have that luxury. I gather my energy and force myself to calm down.

"I'm sorry," I say again, and it's harder than it should be to force those words out of my mouth. It feels weird, like I'm not completely myself, and I wonder if this is part of what it means to be a white witch, learning to control some new variation of my power.

Rule watches me for several seconds until it becomes awkward. That's when I notice the bag on the ground next to his feet, one he evidently dropped when I attacked him. Slowly he reaches down and picks it up. He pulls out two books and extends them to me.

"I saw you almost freak at my grandmother wanting us to wait until in the morning to start looking through the material, so I brought you some," he says.

I stare at the books then back at Rule's face as I take them. "Why would you do that, go against your grandmother for people you just met? Ones who could pose you harm."

"Grandma's never wrong about people. If she thinks you're to be trusted, that's enough for me. Plus, you know, you passed the test."

Ah, yes, the test. I'm still not sure I buy that whole nails of the cross deal, but is it any stranger than the powers a bloodstone possesses? Plus, if it gets me information, I'll go with Fiona's belief in it.

Still, there's a first time for everything, even for Fiona to be wrong in her people assessment. But suddenly I don't want her to be wrong, don't want to give her any reason to regret her trust.

"Thank you."

Rule shifts the bag's strap to his shoulder. "That seems hard for you to say."

"I'm not in a position to have to say it often."

"Not a lot of people on your side?"

"No. Just Egan." And Keller and Toni. That too-familiar pang of loss and guilt punches me in the gut. I miss them both terribly, and at least a dozen times a day I wonder if I made the right decision in leaving them behind without even a goodbye.

And then I remember my mother's broken and drained body, as lifeless as a dried corn husk, and know in the deepest part of me that I had no choice if I wanted to ensure their safety.

"Well, now you've got me," Rule says.

Having someone else in my corner should feel like a victory, but I don't want someone else to worry about becoming collateral damage in a witch war. I already don't like involving Rule and his family long enough to sift through their historical documents, but I have to. They're the only chance I have of finding out what happened in the past and if a white witch might have the power to stop the covens.

I press the books against my chest. "Thanks for the information, but you need to go home."

"Why?" Rule plants his feet and looks as if he doesn't plan on going anywhere anytime soon.

"Because being near us isn't the safest place to be."

"Neither is sitting atop centuries worth of information the world's covens would kill to destroy."

He has a point. "But the covens don't know about that bunker of information, or you and your family would already be toast. The covens do, however, know that Egan and I are out here somewhere bucking authority."

I watch him for a moment and detect something unsaid just beneath the surface.

"Why are you really here?" I ask.

"Because I want to know more, do more. Our family has been on the sidelines for centuries. It's time we did something instead of letting the covens continue to have their way."

I walk in a half-circle around Rule. "And just what do you think you can do? You are powerless. What can you do anyway besides tie herbs in bundles?"

I don't like how ugly and mean I sound, and hate how I can't tell if it's the new, more powerful me talking or just my normal self trying to convince Rule to stay out of harm's way.

"Power comes in different forms," he says.

I shake my head as I stop pacing. "You barely have the right to call yourself a witch. You could no more defend yourself against a coven witch than an average human."

"Is that right?"

I lift a finger and let him see the electric power sparking white there like tiny bolts of lightning before I flick the finger, tossing him back against the wall without even touching him.

"Damn, Jax, quit using your power," Egan hisses from the doorway. "And close this door before you turn the house into a freezer."

My vision darkens as I look at Egan. His startled expression gives me a moment's pause.

Egan looks at Rule and points toward the street. "Go."

This time, Rule doesn't argue. He does pause when he comes abreast of me. "I'm going to help you, whether you like it or not. And I don't think you're going to fry me just to make a point."

For a moment, I'm not so sure of that. But then the idea of having another friend somehow overrides my will to protect Rule and his family. I can't find appropriate words to thank him before he retraces his steps down the path.

When I no longer hear his footfalls, I turn back toward the cottage to find Egan staring hard at me.

"What the hell was that?" he asks.

"What do you mean?"

"You're always the one saying not to use our powers, and trust me, it's been damned hard the past several days, more so than usual. Then you go all sparky-fingers tossing around some dude who just might lead you to some answers before our families make our heads spin like we're in *The Exorcist*."

I press the heel of my hand against my forehead. "I know. I just feel . . . off. Tired and on edge. Maybe it's the white witch power. I just don't know how to harness and control it yet."

"Well, you better figure it out soon before you get us killed."

He's right, but that thought makes me feel like I just slid a little closer to the edge.

I stride into Wiccan Good Herbs the next morning with a renewed determination to end the day with more answers than I begin it. One question has to be answered to my satisfaction before any of the others.

Fiona looks up from where she's replenishing a shelf of herbs. "Good morning, Jax."

"Did you send someone to search our place last night while Egan and I were here?"

"No."

"Are there others like you?"

"Yes, but not in Salem." Her ease in answering with no hesitation convinces me she's telling the truth.

"Well, that means the intruder is someone else, someone with an unknown agenda." I pace across the room. "I've felt like someone has been watching me, but I thought it was Rule. Now I don't think he was the only one."

"You think the person who broke into your cottage has been watching you?"

"Maybe. I don't sense a dark witch's signature, but they might not have used any magic, which would make it more difficult to detect." But a coven member wouldn't have stopped at snooping. They would have waited for Egan and me to return to try to finish what my coven started during the battle at Shiprock. "I don't think it's a dark witch though. It feels different, sort of like you and your family, but not quite the same. Do you know who it might be?"

Fiona shakes her head, her brows knitting in concern. "I'm afraid not, but we'll keep our eyes open for anything unusual."

She finishes her task in silence.

"You're worried," I say.

"I would be a fool not to acknowledge that having you and Egan here is dangerous. You're both powerful, and you evidently have powerful enemies. That puts my family at risk, puts everything our family has gathered over the centuries at risk."

"You want us to leave." Not that I'm going to agree to that. She shakes her head. "No. I think it's imperative that we help you, and you help us. We each have knowledge the other needs. We're stronger together than apart." Fiona looks up and meets my eyes. "But know this. I may not have access to powerful magic like you do, but if I feel like you are a threat to my family, I will do everything in my power to stop you."

My muscles tighten in response to her threat, but I force myself to relax. Another part of me respects her stance, her courage to stand up to a witch she knows could destroy her with next to no effort.

After holding my gaze for several meaningful seconds, Fiona glances toward the street. "So, you left Egan behind today?"

"He's doing his own research." We decided it's safer for him to do some online snooping today, maybe see if there's any buzz in the hunter community about our whereabouts. If the prowler wasn't a member of Fiona's family or the covens, a hunter makes the most sense.

"Something is bothering you," Fiona says.

"Lots of things."

"No, something specific."

I stare at her. "Are you sure you don't have magic?"

She smiles. "Just good old-fashioned intuition."

I tuck my hair back behind my ear and consider how to answer. I don't want to get Rule in trouble for bringing me those books. "Rule had the misfortune of showing up at the cottage right after us last night. I might have been a bit aggressive in confronting him."

"Oh? I saw him this morning. He seems fine to me."

I tell her about how I'd reacted when I'd heard Rule approach the cottage.

"You were understandably wary after discovering the break-in, but I get the feeling this reaction isn't normal for you."

I shake my head. "I don't feel like myself sometimes. I keep thinking it's fatigue or just being jumpy all the time because I'm afraid I won't find a way to protect us before the covens find us. But I don't know."

"You think something changed when you fought your coven and won?"

I shrug. "Maybe."

After Adele comes to mind the shop, Fiona motions for me to follow her into the back room. When she reaches the cupboard, she opens the door and leads the way downstairs.

I halt a couple of steps from the bottom. What had been an orderly room the night before now consists of a bunch of scattered maps and opened books. And in the middle of the research explosion sits Rule.

"Aren't you supposed to be in school?" I don't know why I am being so ugly to him, especially since I feel guilty about how I treated him the night before. He's done nothing but offer me help.

Yes, you do. Despite the fact I still love Keller, something about Rule pulls at me. And that makes me angry.

"Aren't you?" Rule asks without looking up.

"I'm eighteen, graduated."

"No, you're not."

I don't bother trying to convince him.

"It's teacher in-service day," he says, finally answering my question.

I take a deep breath, determined to be more pleasant. I descend the rest of the stairs and approach the table. I run my hand over a pile of loose papers. "How long have you all been working already?"

"When I came down here an hour ago, this one was already at it," Fiona says.

Rule looks up then and meets my gaze for a brief moment, long enough for me to realize he's probably been in this room since he returned from the cottage last night. That knowledge makes me feel like a bitch.

"Found anything yet?" I soften my tone, smoothing away the rough edges.

"We've mainly been refreshing our memories about the families that became the dark covens," Fiona says.

"Yours was the first," Rule says, a hint of accusation in his voice.

Okay, I deserve a bit of payback.

"I didn't know that," I say. But it doesn't surprise me, not if my ancestors were anything like my father.

Rule pushes a weathered ledger toward me. "Seems Olaf Pherson had advocated fighting back against the witch hunts even before he knew about the wells of dark power that existed in the earth."

"Wait. Olaf died in the witch hunts," I say.

"No, he was the leading voice for accepting the dark power so they could fight back."

"Can you blame him? They were killing us for no reason." I wince at how I jump to the defense of a man who'd evidently led the witch families to become the vindictive forces they are today. I just can't seem to keep a lid on my anger lately.

I press my hand against my forehead as I sink into a chair. "I'm sorry. I've not been feeling well."

"I can make you some soothing tea," Fiona offers.

"No offense, but I don't think I'm going to be trying any more of your tea."

To my surprise, Fiona laughs. "I don't blame you."

The laughter lightens the mood, and I breathe a bit easier.

"How did they find out about the dark power, how to even draw upon it?" I ask.

"Someone in one of the other families remembered a story told by his grandmother," Fiona says. "This bit was oral history, so we've never been able to identify who it was."

"But when Olaf heard the story, he became an advocate for tapping into that power," Rule says. "Members of the various families started searching up and down the East Coast for fissures in the earth where the power seeps out to the surface.

Some weren't careful and got themselves killed."

"We encountered some of them, in North Carolina," I say, shivering at the memory of the spirit coven that had almost killed one of my classmates.

Fiona and Rule look at me as if I'm nuts.

"A spirit coven," I explain. "Somehow when they died, they got trapped in that spot. They'd been killing people ever since, until I destroyed them."

Neither Rule nor Fiona speaks for several long seconds, and I worry I've revealed too much about my power.

"We've never heard of such a thing," Fiona finally says.

"Neither had we."

"How did you destroy them?" Rule asks.

"Just blasted them with my power." I make the mistake of looking at Rule. The expression he wears tells me he knows there is more to the story. Maybe I should trust them more. I could be making a huge error by not doing so. "I . . . drew on the power from one of the fissures, too."

Rule's eyes widen, and I sense Fiona tensing.

"Drawing from the fissure gave me enough magic to send my coven members fleeing, but it . . . it scared me."

"And that's when you started feeling different?" Fiona asks. "That edgy, snappish feeling you mentioned?"

I nod. "Soon afterward."

Fiona crosses her hands in front of her on the table. "You messed with something you didn't understand."

"If I hadn't, I'd be dead right now," I say. "So would Egan, as well as some people who weren't witches. I couldn't let that happen."

Fiona and Rule stare at me for a prolonged, uncomfortable moment before Fiona nods. "Somehow you were able to manage it."

"Have you ever heard of anything like that?" I ask.

She shakes her head. "No. I've never heard of anyone drawing on that magic since the days of the Salem trials. Certainly not anyone who was able to control it so that it didn't twist them into something worse than they were before."

"Sometimes I wonder," I say, wondering about how off I've felt since that night. Could be anxiety, fatigue, loss. Or is it something else? Did I open a can of very ugly worms?

Rule leans back in his chair and crosses his arms. "How did you find this spirit coven?"

"By accident. Someone we knew had a wreck on the way back from a dance. When we stopped to help her, Egan and I sensed witches. Only we figured out they were dead witches."

"This girl you helped, she wasn't a witch?" Fiona asks.

I don't answer immediately. Something inside me is whispering that these two are asking too many questions, that they pose a threat. But the person I've always been doesn't believe that. I want to believe in the good of people. As I stare at Rule and his grandmother, I realize they are what I might have been had my ancestors not made the wrong decision. Because of that long-ago action, I might never be a simple, harmless witch, but I can certainly try to befriend them. Emulate them.

"No. Egan and I fled our covens and tried to live a normal life. We had non-witch friends." I lower my gaze to the tabletop and wonder what Keller is doing right now. Is he missing me? Or is he so angry about my abrupt departure that he's moved on? My heart aches at that thought.

"Tried?" Rule asks.

I raise my gaze to meet his. "Turns out it was harder than we expected."

"Did you hurt someone?"

I shake my head. "Not like you're thinking. In fact, we left so that people wouldn't get hurt."

I sense that Rule and Fiona have countless more questions. "We came close to getting them killed because they cared about us." I swallow past a lump in my throat, the same lump that always forms when I think about Keller and Toni being kidnapped by my father. The memory of seeing Toni tossed through the air like she weighed no more than a marble. I blink against tears. The worst is the image seared into my brain of Keller inside the Siphoning Circle, the circle of rocks that allows a witch's power to inflict unimaginable pain on the person inside. The same type of circle where my mother died.

"We had no choice but to leave to protect them, to find out as much as we can about the covens' past. I have to know more about that power I drew into myself, if there's a way we can maybe take all that dark magic away from the covens."

I shift in my seat and pull a book toward me. I glance at the title, another history of the witch trials but one I didn't see in the local library. "There's a part of me that understands why the covens did what they did. It was a natural reaction to the threat against their lives, the anger at having lost family members and friends for no reason. I took in that same power to protect my friends, and I'm afraid it will corrupt me. Maybe it already has."

Rule reaches across the table and places his hand over mine. "I don't think you're like them." His words and his hand feel warm and reassuring, and I nearly turn my hand over and entwine my fingers with his. Only the thought of Keller holding me close gives me the strength to pull away.

Instead, I focus my attention on the cover of the book in front of me. When I open it, I see that the pages inside are handwritten in flowing script.

"That's an accounting of what really happened during the time of the trials," Fiona says. "Our ancestor compiled information from members of all the families that fled rather than become dark covens. Perhaps you should read that before anything else."

I've read coven histories, of course, but recent experience with my family has shown that not everything Egan and I were told while growing up is the truth. So I take Fiona's advice and start reading. It takes me several minutes to get used to the script, but then I delve into a past that shaped me centuries before I was born.

The old pages reveal that the dissenters, the families that refused to form dark covens, tried to convince the coven families that tapping into something they didn't understand was too dangerous. That they should just maintain their innocence of any wrongdoing and wait until the hysteria subsided.

Fools. Something inside me spits the word. History had

proven that swearing one's innocence of witchcraft did no good whatsoever. I hate to admit it, but part of me understands why the witches decided to take matters into their own hands. You can only get beaten down for so long before you are compelled to fight back.

As I flip pages and read, I feel as if I'm taking a trip back in time, experiencing those frightening days as if I'd been there. Once the witches figured out how to take the dark power into themselves safely, they faced an unforeseen consequence. Suddenly, Salem was much too small to contain so many witches with that much power. Fights broke out, some deadly, over territory and who should be in charge. I shake my head and think about how they sound like modern-day gangs.

Someone named Nathaniel Hillman recognized that they'd end up tearing each other apart if they didn't spread out. That was the beginning of assigning territories to different covens. Being the architect of this plan, Hillman assigned his own family to Boston, the closest coven to Salem. The others agreed, many of them wanting to get as far away from the bad memories Salem held as they could.

Halfway through the book, I finally look up to find that Fiona has left the room at some point. Only Rule remains, and he's watching me.

"How long have you been staring at me?" I ask.

"A while. You can tell a lot by looking at a person's expressions when they're unaware they're being observed."

"And what do you think you know about me now?"

He points toward the book I'm reading. "That some of what you're reading is new to you."

"That shouldn't be a surprise."

Rule shrugs. "We have no idea what's discussed within the covens."

"Certainly no mention of witches without powers."

"That's good. Maybe the knowledge of us has been lost over the years."

For his sake, he better hope so.

"What have you been reading?"

Rule lifts the paper on the top of the stack in front of him. "Some observations of the newly formed coven members. Their acts of retribution against those who'd killed witches, overheard snippets of conversation."

"Like what?"

He lowers his gaze to the crinkled paper and begins to read. "My daughter and her friend have become the bane of my existence. They have had second thoughts, ones that they are sharing with too many of our neighbors. I fear I shall have to do something regrettable." Rule lowers the paper. "That was from Reginald Davenport, the head of one of the new covens. There's a newspaper account here somewhere dated about a month later reporting that Penelope Davenport and three of her friends disappeared from the edge of town. The official line was they were captured by bandits or Indians, but I suspect ol' Papa Davenport might have 'done something regrettable.'"

"I doubt he regretted it very much. It's been my experience the covens don't experience regret."

"But you're a member of a coven, and I'd wager you've experienced it," he says. "Maybe recently."

"I don't know why, call it an aberration, a recessive gene, whatever, but there is occasionally a coven witch who doesn't fit the mold."

"How many?"

I hesitate, thinking how pitiful the answer will sound in the face of more than three hundred years of witch history. "I know of three. Egan, myself, and . . . my mother."

"Your mother? She fled with you?"

I swallow against the lump forming in my throat. "Not now. She tried, several years ago, but she was caught." Might as well get it all out there because Rule will just keep asking questions. And I want them to know, really know, how committed I am to neutralizing the covens. "The covens do not allow defection, so they killed her. She died a horrible, agonizing death as my sister and I watched. And no, my sister did not flee with me either. She's still fully within the coven fold."

"I'm sorry." His words ring genuine, not with false

condolence. After a few quiet moments, he speaks again. "That's why you want to take away the covens' power, isn't it? So they can't do that to anyone else?"

"Yes. And the fact that I want to be free, to not have to live in hiding or constantly on the run like a fugitive." I pause and stare at my hands for a moment, considering the enormous well of power there at my fingertips. "But it's so much more than that. No one should have this kind of power. What happened to me at Shiprock, it makes me wonder if there's a way to maybe reverse it."

"You'd do that, give up your magical powers?"

I look up and meet his eyes. "If it meant the covens could no longer hurt anyone, yes, in a heartbeat."

If it means people like Keller and Toni will no longer be in danger, I'll give up my life.

Chapter Four

By the time I finish reading the book, I feel as if my butt has adhered to the wooden chair. When I close the book and stretch, I notice Rule has his cheek propped against his upturned palm, and his eyes are closed.

"You should go to bed," I say.

His eyes pop open. "What?"

"You're exhausted. Go get some sleep."

He lifts his head from his hand and blinks several times. "Nothing a good strong cup of coffee won't cure."

"How long have you been up?"

"Not as long as you think. I did sleep last night." He pushes his chair away from the table and stands. "Come on. I'll buy you a cup of coffee."

"That's not necessary."

"You're going to sit there and tell me some caffeine won't help right now? That a walk down the street won't work out the kinks?"

Both of those things sound wonderful right now, and I find myself smiling at him. "I didn't say that."

All the way up the stairs and down the street to the Strong Brew Coffeehouse, I tell myself I'm not doing anything wrong, that I can't cheat on someone I already left. Even if I haven't left Keller in my heart.

When the barista gives us our coffees, we make our way toward a window that overlooks the town's main pedestrian mall. I shiver at the sight of the bundled-up figures walking back and forth, pausing in front of shop windows.

"You're not used to the cold, are you?" Rule asks.

"No. I'm pretty sure hell is cold instead of hot."

He laughs, and it's a pleasant sound that draws me a little

closer to him.

"Where are you from originally?" he asks.

I take a sip of coffee, hoping to ward off some of the chill that's settled in my bones on the walk to the coffeehouse. "You don't know that already?"

"Our family lost track of some of the covens after they left this area, as the country expanded and more cities were built. We kept our attention focused on preserving the history and watching Salem, where everything started."

I place my cup on the table and wrap my hands around it. "Miami."

"And from there you ran to North Carolina?"

"It seemed like a good idea at the time." I run my fingertip along the cup's handle, remembering how much I loved my short time in Baker Gap and yearning to return.

"And you want to go back," he says.

"What makes you say that?"

"You get this faraway look of regret when you mention it."

I sigh and look out the window again. "I just realized, yet again, that there will be no normal life for me, or Egan, until the threat of coven punishment isn't hanging over our heads. Not until we find a way to keep the covens from hurting anyone."

"What will they do to you if they find you?"

"You don't want to know."

Rule reaches across the table and places his hand atop mine. "I do."

His touch feels wrong, so I slip my hand away and lay it in my lap.

"They'll make me wish I could die quickly." I'm not up to describing the Siphoning Circle and how my power would be drained from me, and then my very life, inch by agonizing inch until I scream for mercy like my mother had, a mercy the covens are unable or unwilling to offer.

For a couple of minutes, he doesn't ask me anything else, instead allowing me to enjoy my coffee. But I sense more questions are lying in wait. So I ask one instead. "Have you read everything that's in that room?"

"At some point, yes. But it's too much to remember."

I lean forward, my forearms against the top of the table. "But you would remember if there was something there that could defeat the covens?"

"Yes, but I might not recognize it even if I saw it. I doubt it would come right out and say it in so many words."

I sigh. "It's going to take us forever to get through everything."

"Maybe we'll get lucky."

I shake my head. "Luck and I haven't been on the best of terms lately."

When I finish my coffee, Rule points at my cup. "You want some more?"

"No, I'm good. We should get back to work."

"How about we go for a drive first?"

"Rule . . ."

"I just thought you might like to see your ancestors' property. It's not that far out of town toward Danvers."

That does hold more appeal than burying myself back in that basement full of old papers. "Okay."

Rule retrieves his car from the herb shop and drives out of town. It only takes about fifteen minutes for his series of turns to bring us to a piece of property lined with trees down one side.

"This is it," he says. "Where the Phersons lived."

And died. Innocent members of my family were struck down right here. A shiver runs down my back at the terror they must have felt, the injustice of their impending deaths. It contrasts so much with the peaceful scene before me now.

"You okay?" Rule asks.

"It's just so real sitting here staring at it." I shake my head. "I've heard about my ancestors all my life, but after what I've learned recently I wonder how much of it was true."

"Members of your family did die here at the hands of zealots. If nothing else you've been told was true, that much is."

I wonder how I would have reacted if I'd seen my family slaughtered for no reason, a family that was good and kind. My stomach turns. I do know how that feels, and for a time I'd wanted to strike back. Fight evil with evil. But something inside me recoils at that. Is that the part I thought might have made me a white witch in Baker Gap? Something in me that wants to fight evil even when some of my thoughts and feelings seem evil, too?

"It still didn't justify what happened as a result." I get out of the car, and despite the cold wind I start walking across the rolling piece of land.

The darkness inside me vibrates with the need to punish, as if it can hear those long-ago screams, and I wonder if my ancestors felt that same roiling need for retribution.

My breath catches, causing me to pause, as the darkness shifts inside me. It feels different, darker, almost . . . separate. Is being here in this place amping up my dark magic, causing it to suppress whatever light magic I might have accessed at Shiprock? Or was the potential for being a white witch lost that night, burned away in that one furious display? Have I instead awakened something much worse?

Fiona's words come back to me. *You messed with something you don't understand.*

I start moving again, forcing myself to breathe deeply and slowly. I spend half an hour walking, and Rule lets me have space. Only when I can barely feel my ears and nose do I start back toward the car. Rule slips into the driver's seat and starts the engine as soon as I turn his direction. By the time I reach the car, the heat is blasting out of the vents.

"Thanks," I say, indicating the heat.

"You're welcome. Wish I'd thought to bring some extra coffee along."

"It's okay. I don't think I need to be any more wired than I already am." I want to blame the coffee for the jittery feeling zipping through my body, but I know better. I can drink a barrel of coffee and not experience the edginess I feel now.

"So, are you and Egan a couple?"

Rule's question comes so totally out of nowhere that I stare at him.

"I mean, you're both witches. Evidently the only two to defect. Would make sense."

"Not in this lifetime," I say. Hope flickers in his eyes, and I have no choice but to squash it. "But I'm not in the dating market."

He watches me for a few seconds. "That's who you left North Carolina to protect, isn't it? Someone you cared about?"

I consider denying it then wonder why. "Yes, and friends. People who aren't equipped to deal with the covens."

Rule nods and reaches toward the gearshift.

My hand shoots out and tightens around his wrist before I realize why. "Wait."

"What is it?" he asks.

I lift my hand and motion for him to be quiet. There it is, the odd vibration I felt before when I was sure I was being watched. It's the same as what was left behind by the person who broke into the cottage.

"Someone is watching us." More than that. Though I don't recognize the signature, and it isn't full strength, I get the distinct sensation it's a witch.

Electric power sizzles at my fingertips as I burst out of the car. I scan the surrounding area as I stalk past the front of the car, toward the source of the signature. I let the power build until it's arcing between my hands like bolts of blue-white lightning.

"Jax."

Rule makes the mistake of touching my arm, and the power vibrating off of my body sends him flying. He curses as he lands on his back. I turn my head and look at him. When he straightens and returns my gaze, his eyes widen.

"What the hell?" he says.

In the moment it takes me to shift my attention back to the watcher, they're gone. I no longer sense anyone or anything resembling a witch signature. Something in me roars in frustration and has me spinning toward Rule. He caused this, the loss of my prey.

Prey? The word shakes me, and it takes me a moment to pull my magic in and calm down enough to speak.

"Are you sure there isn't anyone else like you and your family here in Salem?" I ask without looking at him.

Rule gets up from where he landed. "There shouldn't be. Hasn't been in a very long time."

"Is there anyone local who might take an interest in me? Someone who knows about witches?"

"Are you kidding? Witchcraft is mostly just the thing that keeps the tourists coming and spending their money."

I turn halfway back toward him and point in the opposite direction. "I'm not kidding. Someone was watching us, someone who was way too interested in us, someone who left awfully fast when I detected them."

Rule scans the line of trees at the edge of the property then the rest of the horizon. "Maybe they were just surprised to see someone on this property."

I'm shaking my head before he even finishes. "No, it's more than that. And I don't like it."

"Well, they're gone now. Maybe you scared the crap out of them."

I stare at his profile. "Do I scare you?"

He glances at me before returning his attention to our surroundings. "You've attacked me twice in twenty-four hours. What do you think?"

"You could have left."

"And how would I explain that when I got back? 'Oh, Jax? I left her out in the country to fend for herself against an unknown stalker because she scares me.'" He looks at me. "Call me crazy, but I'm not that kind of guy."

I shake my head. "Crazy," I mutter.

He smiles a little as I turn away and look up at the sky and its waning wintry light. I've always hated when the days shorten, stretching the night to interminable lengths. Now, with cold added to the equation, I don't know how I'm going to get through the winter.

With another deep breath, I feel the last of my dangerous edge calm. Unable to meet Rule's gaze, I walk back to the car and slide into the passenger's seat. He slips quietly into the driver's side and stares out the windshield for what seems like forever.

"I could have taken care of myself, you know," I say. "Made

my own way back."

"I'm sure you could." He meets my gaze. "Only part of you scares me." He points toward the front of the car. "The part that was out there, that slammed me against the side of your cottage."

"And yet you willingly spend time alone with me?"

"Yes." Something about the way he says it makes me want to squirm. "The fact that you left your coven tells me that those slips are not really you. You're looking for answers not only for yourself but to benefit everyone by ridding the world of the covens' powers. You may be struggling, but I see conviction in you."

I slowly shake my head. "You are entirely too observant."

He smiles. "In the genetic code, I guess." He sobers when he looks away. "Do you think it could have been a hunter watching us?"

"No. I got the sense it was a witch, but something felt off. The energy level wasn't the same as a coven witch, and I barely get any vibration off of you and your family at all. It was somewhere in between, like what I've felt a couple of other times since coming to Salem. It doesn't make any sense, but then before coming here we didn't know your kind existed. I have to wonder what else is out there that we don't know about."

This time when Rule reaches for the ignition to start the car, I don't stop him. "We'll ask my grandmother about it when we get back."

I don't hold out much hope that Fiona will have miraculously remembered who my observer might be. I know, deep down, that the only way I'm going to find out is a direct confrontation. I flex my fingers, the tips of them growing warm with my power. Whoever is out there, I'll find them. And they're going to give me some answers, one way or another.

As I expect, Fiona still doesn't have any explanation for the feeling I experienced at the old Pherson property. And we don't find any during the next several days of examining the contents of the history texts.

After a week of work, I crawl into bed one night feeling defeated. I've learned a lot about the covens' history through first-person accounts, all of it enlightening but ultimately not useful.

My eyes are already drooping by the time my head hits the pillow, and sleep drags me under like a hungry beast.

I stand in the middle of the forest clearing at Shiprock with Keller. He walks slowly toward me, and with each step I feel calmer, more like myself. It's like his presence erases my darkness, leaving only the bright light of a white witch behind. I feel like Yvaine in *Stardust*, glowing so bright that the night lights up with my happiness.

When he reaches me and lifts his hand to my cheek, I smile with a pure, consuming joy. I know with absolute certainty that our love is more powerful than any darkness. I don't know why I ever worried about the covens or their dark magic. We can defeat it.

But in the blink of an eye, we're surrounded by not only my coven but all of them. Dark witches stretch out in waves as far as I can see, and potent fear slams into me. All those dark witches point their power at Keller, bringing my greatest fear to life. His body jerks in pain as they attack them. I scream like a wounded animal, and all my light turns pitch black as I focus all my power toward the covens and blast them.

I come awake with a violent jerk. It takes me a moment to realize Egan has tossed me from my bed and is beating out the flames licking at my sheets. All I can do is stare as the dream fades to be replaced with reality.

When Egan finishes extinguishing my bed, he spins toward me. "What is going on? You set your bed on fire."

I shake my head, trying to make sense of what just happened. "I was dreaming about fighting the covens." I lift my hands and look at my fingertips. They are still warm from my discharge of power. I start shaking. "What is happening to me?"

Egan sinks down beside me on the floor and does something he's never done before, pulls me into his arms. It isn't like when Keller did it, it's more like a brother, but I find some comfort in the embrace.

Two days later, I look up from reading the pompous ramblings of some old blowhard who'd been determined to rid the earth of the scourge of witchcraft. Ironic since one of those pre-trial witches had used herbs to cure his rather nasty chest congestion. Ungrateful bastard.

I scan the room, not for the first time wondering if the missing page to the Beginning Book is somewhere in this stockpile of information. The more time that ticks away, the more desperate I feel. Eventually, the covens will figure out where Egan and I are and return to Salem. Won't they? Or is it more than bad memories that keep the covens away? It can't be anything too dangerous because Egan and I are still upright and functioning.

Egan's phone pings as he stands, and he slides it out of his jean pocket. He stops walking, and I detect a spike in his anxiety level.

"What is it?" I ask.

It takes him a moment to respond, as if he didn't hear me. When he meets my eyes, his are pained. "It's Keller and Toni. They're missing."

Chapter Five

My heart drops like a stone. "What do you mean they're missing?"

Egan holds up his phone. "I set up alerts for their names in case anything showed up on any of my sources. They didn't show up for school two days ago, and no one has seen them since."

Fear and anger propel me out of my chair and wake the darkness within me. I grip the edge of the table so hard that I wouldn't be surprised if it disintegrated between my fingers. I sense Egan's anger escalating, too.

Rule stands and walks slowly toward me. Adele grabs his arm, but he shakes her off.

"Fight it," he says, and I know instantly what he means. Rule may not have the same sensory abilities as Egan and me, but anyone would be able to see that I want to lash out.

And who could blame me? If my coven has taken Keller and Toni, I don't want to fight my new levels of power. I want to use everything I have to get them back and punish their abductors.

Rule takes another step toward me. "You know the light is more powerful than the dark," he says, his voice soothing and even. "You said so yourself."

His presence doesn't have the same instant effect that Keller's had in my dream, but his words are enough to clear my thoughts a bit. I shove the darkness down and loosen my grip on the table. I push past Rule toward Egan.

When he looks at me, he's poised to fight. His eyes are darker than any human's should ever be, but that's normal for a coven witch on the verge of calling up his magic.

"We have to hold it together and find them," I say.

For a moment, it's like he can't even hear me past his anger and visceral need to protect Toni. But then he blinks, and the darkness begins to fade from his eyes.

Fiona steps toward us but keeps her eyes focused on Egan. "Did you draw power from the fissure, too?"

He looks up. "No."

"I'm the only one who did," I say. "But we do seem to be somehow connected now. We're more aware of each other's emotions, particularly when it stirs our power."

"Interesting." Fiona looks at me. "Is there anything else you'd like to share? Anything that might lead us in the right direction to figure out what's going on with you two?"

I consider the last bit of information Egan and I hold. He knows what I'm thinking because he nods when I look at him. He loves Toni, and she's in danger. He'll do whatever is necessary to get her safely back, even if he ends up walking away again.

"Have you ever heard of the Beginning Book?"

"The book that supposedly was forged at the time of the covens' formation?" Fiona asks.

"Yes."

"It's a myth."

"It's not. We know that because we have it."

For the first time since I met her, Fiona looks shocked. "I never thought it was real."

"We didn't either until Egan found it for sale in a little bookstore in West Texas that was going out of business. The covens believe it was lost, but someone evidently hid it."

"Why?" Rule asks.

"We're not sure. Most of what is in it are things we already knew, but there is a page missing. My gut tells me there is information on that page that the covens don't want known. Either the page was destroyed, or it was taken for safekeeping by someone who was at odds with the covens."

"Can I see it?" Fiona asks.

I hesitate for a moment then walk toward my chair. I open my bag and pull out the Beginning Book. I take it everywhere with me, unwilling to leave it vulnerable. I hate to think what might have happened if it had been in the cottage when our intruder started snooping around.

I place the plain black book on the table. Fiona hesitates as if she's afraid to approach it.

It's Rule who steps forward and runs his hand over the cover. "I've seen this before."

"That's impossible," Egan says.

"Not this book but one that looks like it." He walks to the back of the room, to an area we've not reached yet in our examinations. After some searching, he pulls a black book from the shelf and carries it back to the table. When he places it beside the Beginning Book, my breath catches.

They are exactly the same with the exception of the faint, indented initials in the corner of the cover. I step closer and turn both books to face me. Where the Beginning Book has a small "BB" in the corner, its twin has an "EB". It's not until I open the cover and read the words on the first page that I know why.

"The Ending Book," I say.

No one responds. When I look up they're giving me various looks of surprise and confusion. "What?"

"How did you know what that said?" Rule asks.

"Um, because it says it right here on the page."

"Jax, none of us can read that," he says. "We can't even identify the language."

"That's crazy." I shift my gaze to Egan, but he shakes his head.

"I can't read it either," he says.

My legs suddenly go wobbly, and I sink into my chair.

Adele is the one to step forward and speak. "If you can read this, then you have to tell us what it says. You said it was the Ending Book. I can't be the only one thinking this could be the thing we've been searching for all these years."

"And it was right here under our noses the entire time," Rule says as he stares at the Ending Book with a mixture of awe and caution.

"We just weren't the ones meant to understand it." Fiona

sits across from me and places her weathered hands atop mine. "You are, dear. This is something very big, and you are at the center of it."

I don't know whether to be excited, nauseated or a bit of both. But if this book holds the answers to making sure Keller and Toni are safe, I'll do whatever it says.

Fiona refuses to let the Ending Book leave the basement. I sit and read with the full awareness that everyone else is watching me. Oh, they do their own research, but every few moments their attention wanders to me. It makes it hard to concentrate.

Even when everyone gets tired, I keep reading. Adele orders pizzas and brings them downstairs so we can keep going. She's every bit as interested in what the book says as everyone else. Several times I'm tempted to share something I read, but I decide to wait until I finish. I need to absorb everything and see how it all fits together.

At some point, I must fall asleep because I wake up to the smell of coffee and a hand placed gently on my back. I lift my head from the table aware I likely have crease marks on my cheek. As I blink away sleep, I see Rule slip into the chair next to me. A scan of the room shows that Fiona and Adele must have gone to bed. Egan is sacked out on an old couch in the corner, a thin ledger open on his chest.

"How long have I been asleep?" I ask.

Rule finally lets his hand slip away from my back, and for a moment I'm sorry to lose the warmth. But then I remember Keller, and my heart squeezes painfully. Where is he? Is he okay? Will I ever see him again? I feel so useless, but I know the best way to help him is to find a way to defeat the covens.

"About six hours. I figured you'd want to get back to work," Rule says.

I watch him for several seconds. "You are really good at this observation thing."

He smiles, but it dims when he shifts his gaze away. "I'm sorry about your friends. Keller, he's the one you care about?"

I swallow hard. "Yes. But I can't be with him."

"Because of your coven?"

I nod. "And, honestly, I'm too much of a danger to him in my current state. To you, too. To anyone until I learn to control whatever power is inside me now."

He shrugs. "I can handle it."

I sigh. "You sound like him, thinking he can handle more than he can."

"Maybe you underestimate us," Rule says as he wraps my hand in his.

"Maybe you all underestimate how much glee a coven would take in ripping you to shreds. Trust me when I say they're not into killing people quickly."

"She's right about that," Egan says.

I jump and slide my hand away from Rule's. I don't meet either his or Egan's gazes, not wanting to see the possible hurt in Rule's or the accusation in Egan's.

But you haven't done anything. You deserve a friend, don't you?

It isn't that ugly, selfish something speaking to me this time but rather my heart. Despite being around people every day, loneliness plagues me. Keller is the only person who can fill that empty spot, so it's possible I might feel this way for the rest of my life. I blink several times to keep tears from falling at that thought.

"We appreciate the help," Egan continues as he strides toward the table. "This is something Jax and I will have to handle ourselves." His voice sounds raw. I'm not sure if that is from sleep or his worry over Toni. I know it's killing him to not take more action, but he has enough sense to know it'd be a suicide run if he went after any of the covens alone.

"Maybe not." I run my hand over the Ending Book. "I'm not finished yet, but there's something in here that gives me hope that we might not be alone in this." I flip back several pages and reread a passage that made my heart beat wildly the night before. "It seems that there were some witches who took in the dark power but immediately regretted it and advocated for finding a way to put it back. Some of them were killed by the newly formed dark witches. Others fled." I glance at Rule.

"This is all new information to me," he says.

"You remember when we were reading about Penelope Davenport and her friends disappearing, and her father calling them the bane of his existence?" I ask.

"Yeah."

"There are references to something called the Bane in here. I think it's the group of witches who wanted to change back." I look at Egan. "What if they still exist, the Bane, the descendants of those original witches? Maybe we could persuade them to help us."

"Nice thought, but how do we find them even if they are still around? They've obviously kept themselves well hidden if even the observers don't know about them."

"I don't know. I still have some to read."

Egan motions toward the book. "Then get to it. We have people to find, and the better armed we are when we do it, the more likely none of us end up barbecued."

My muscles tense at the thought of fighting my coven again, of possibly having to fight even more covens. There's a very real possibility Egan and I won't survive another encounter, but I'm not going to give up, not when Keller and Toni may be in danger. I open the book and start to read. If I can find these Bane witches, maybe they can help us learn to control our powers better. Maybe they will know something about white witches, if I am one and what that means.

The boys disappear upstairs for more coffee and some breakfast, but I remain in the basement reading. With only a few pages left, I hit information that elevates my heart rate. I can't turn the pages fast enough. I leap to my feet to run upstairs just as the guys and Fiona start back down.

"What?" Egan says when he sees the expression on my face.

"It's true," I say, holding the Ending Book to my chest. "There is such a thing as a white witch. Only a white witch has the power to stop the covens."

Egan takes another step down toward me. "How?"

My excitement deflates some. "That I don't know. The

book says it's too dangerous to have all the information in one place, that the final piece of the puzzle is somewhere that is alike but not the same."

"The missing page of the Beginning Book," Egan says.

I nod. "I think so."

Egan growls in frustration and stalks across the room, running his fingers through his hair. "That gets us back to square one."

I sense his anger mixed with helplessness and fear a moment before he punches the wall. I wince but don't tell him to calm down. I know exactly how he feels. Like we're wading through information in slow motion while also vibrating with the need to do something to find Toni and Keller. Everyone stands still, silent as Egan braces his palms against the wall and hangs his head.

"Are you okay?" Fiona asks him when he seems to calm.

I sense a flicker of appreciation in him for Fiona's concern. Unlike me, he's never had a parent who has shown him love. His mother is one of the coldest witches I've ever met. She makes Cruella DeVille look like a saint.

He takes a moment but finally nods, pushes himself away from the wall and faces us. "What do we do now? Much as I'd like to storm the castle, so to speak, I don't like the idea of ending up dead."

I look over the tons of history we've sifted through in the past several days and consider how much more we know now than when we arrived in Salem. "We need to figure out if the Bane are still around. If they'll help us."

"And how do we do that?"

I gesture toward the extensive library around us. "We need to figure out the names of those other girls who disappeared, then find everyone in this area that has those family names, as well as Davenport."

"Easy enough with Google. But then what? We just go up and ask, 'Hey, are you a Bane witch?'" Egan asks.

"No, smartass. But we can watch them, see where they go and what they do. Maybe even test them to see if they have any powers." I place the Ending Book on the table. "Some of us need to stay here to research. But I've been down here so long I'm beginning to feel like a mole. We know Penelope Davenport's name. I'm going to visit some of the area cemeteries and see if I can find her."

"Hold that thought," Egan says as he slides into a chair and pulls out his laptop. "I'll do a cemetery search."

"But there's nothing in anything we've read that says Penelope was ever found," Rule says. "What makes you think she's buried somewhere nearby?"

"The covens left Salem soon after they were formed. The pre-trial witches stayed, so maybe the Bane did, too. And if they did, they have to be buried somewhere."

After several minutes of searching, Egan hands me a list of five Davenports buried in or close to Salem. "No Penelope though," he says.

"It's worth looking anyway," I say. "It might give us nothing, but I've got to *do* something or go crazy."

"I'll go with you," Rule says. "I know the local cemeteries pretty well."

I nod then look at Egan. "Ready to put your mad computer skills to work again?"

Egan laces his fingers and cracks his knuckles.

"See if there's any new information on Keller and Toni, or anything else that might be useful to us," I say.

He looks like he's been released from prison. To him, sifting through all these old papers in a windowless basement probably is like prison. Give him a computer and various gadgets any day.

"I've got to get out of here, too," he says. "I'm going back to the cottage for a while."

After Egan heads up the stairs, Fiona steps in front of Rule and me before we can leave. "Be careful."

Rule looks surprised by her words, and honestly I am, too.

"Is something wrong?" I ask.

"I feel like the more we learn, the more dangerous things become," she says. "Something is nagging at me. And even pre-trial witches had pretty good intuition."

"We'll be careful," I say. "I won't take Rule into any dangerous situations."

Rule doesn't look too happy that he's being protected, but he has enough sense to keep his mouth shut. At least until he and I get outside. "You don't have to treat me like a baby."

"I'm not. I'm treating you like a guy who has no power to protect himself if the crap really hits the fan."

Rule goes quiet and doesn't say anything else until we reach the Old Burying Point Cemetery a short distance from the herb shop. He stops before we pass through the gate and points toward several stone benches placed in a U shape next to a low, stone wall.

"This memorial is dedicated to the people the history books say died in the Salem witch trials," he says. "We all know there should be a lot more, but at least it's something."

I walk slowly past the benches, reading the inscriptions in the granite. Bridget Bishop, Hanged, July 10, 1692. Rebecca Nurse, Hanged, July 19, 1692. Martha Carrier, John Proctor, and fifteen others, all innocent and hanged. And then there's the one that always makes me shiver. Giles Corey, Sept. 19, 1692, pressed to death. I can't imagine the pain and suffering endured by the old man as rock upon rock was stacked onto his body until the combined weight finally killed him. All for refusing to enter a plea to a hysteria-fed charge.

I wonder what the thousands of tourists visiting this spot each year would think if they knew how many other markers should be sitting in this spot with similar inscriptions.

"If those witch hunters had only known what evil they were breeding," I say.

"Ironic that their actions brought about the very thing they thought they were getting rid of."

"Did your family lose anyone?" I ask, looking up at the boy beside me and feeling myself grow more attached to him. Not the way I am with Keller, but I definitely care what happens to Rule.

"A many times great-grandmother."

I sigh. "And yet your family was strong enough to resist letting revenge blacken their souls."

"What your family did back then isn't your fault," he says.

"I know." I do, really I do. But that doesn't make me feel any less guilty about bearing the Pherson name. "Come on."

After locating the graves of the five people on Egan's list at the first three cemeteries we visit, we don't find any Davenports in the next four. I do note the names of a couple of women who were supposedly witches, though in a town like Salem having a "witch" in a graveyard is just good business.

The afternoon light is waning when Rule makes his way down a winding lane to the Wildwood Cemetery, a final resting place for about twenty souls off the beaten path.

"I haven't been out here since I was a little kid. I think it was a Cub Scouts outing where we cleaned the plant growth away from the stones."

A smile stretches my lips. "Cub Scouts, huh?"

"Always be prepared. Think about it. The scouting motto matches up pretty well with my family's."

"True."

Rule parks and we get out of the car. He pushes open the wooden gate. It looks like it's gotten a new coat of red paint recently.

The absolute quiet of the place hits me the moment we pass through the gate. And while there are hundreds of old graves in Salem, these feel ancient somehow. We don't speak as we wander past the stone markers, some of them so old that the words have faded away while others are well kept, their ornate designs still clear. I wonder if we might pass by Penelope's grave and not even know it.

As we near the back of the cemetery, I notice a large crypt in one corner. The darkness inside me coils like a snake preparing to strike. I stop and try to take a deep breath. It's much harder than it should be. Rule doesn't notice because he's walked ahead. I try to fight panic as I realize this darkness is different. Is this what I'd pulled from the earth at Shiprock?

I force myself to begin walking again, but with each step I

take toward the crypt, the darkness grows more agitated.

Rule looks back at me. He must notice something in my expression because his reflects concern. "What is it?"

"There's something about that crypt. I feel pulled toward it. Pulled and repelled at the same time."

When we get close, I notice the name etched above the door. Davenport. My heart starts beating triple time. Have we found Penelope? And if so, what does it mean that I feel drawn to the woman's final resting place?

I walk around the entire crypt but see no other indication of who is entombed inside. Other than the surname, the only thing I see is an ornate sun carved in the massive stone door. I lift my hand toward the carving, and the darkness inside me writhes and twists so much that I double over.

"Jax, what's wrong?" Rule wraps his arm around my back, but the contact only serves to upset me more. Pain stabs at my insides, making me cry out. Despite the chill in the air, sweat breaks out all over my body, and my breath starts coming fast.

"Something doesn't want me here for some reason," I say, my voice strained.

"Let's go." Rule tries to guide me back toward the cemetery entrance, but I pull out of his grasp.

"No. I need to stay." Something in the deepest core of my being, something even deeper than the pain, makes me lift my hand toward the sun carving. But as soon as my fingers touch it, I scream and snatch them back. Smoke rises from my fingertips where the stone burned me.

Rule grabs my hand and examines the reddened skin. "Let's get you back so my grandmother can fix this."

The pain strikes again, causing me to bend backward as if possessed. Maybe I am. Maybe I truly do have a demon inside me.

Rule uses more strength than I would have credited him with to drag me away from the crypt and the cemetery. When I struggle against him, doing my best not to blast him with my magic, he turns me forcefully away so that I can no longer see the crypt.

He ushers me into the car then runs to the driver's side. The car's tires spit gravel as he speeds away from the cemetery. I expect the pain to settle as we drive away, but it continues to roil and bite and make its unwanted presence known. I don't examine it too closely. I'm afraid of what I might find.

Chapter Six

"What the hell happened?" Egan asks as he storms out of the cottage.

I look up from where Rule is helping me up the cobblestone walkway. "I think I found Penelope Davenport."

Egan halts in his tracks and simply stares at me as if one thing has nothing to do with the other.

"You think we could go inside before she crumples?" Rule asks.

"I'm fine, really." But I wasn't only minutes before.

Egan leads the way inside. Once across the front threshold, I step away from Rule.

"Here." Rule extends a tube of ointment he'd gotten from the shop for my burned fingers.

I take it. "Thank you, for everything." He really is turning out to be a good friend, and that scares me. Someone else I fear will get hurt because of my coven's pursuit of me.

"Someone going to tell me what's going on?" Egan asks.

I fill him in on what happened at the cemetery.

"Now that's just flipping weird," he says when I'm finished.

"That's one way of putting it," I say. "And it makes it even more important to find out if any of the Bane are still alive, and where they are. If that's Penelope's crypt, it's somehow infused with some strong magic that really doesn't like coven witches."

Egan runs his hand back over his hair. "What we need, one more thing to worry about."

I detect the change in his voice and realize that I miss the old, carefree Egan. "Did you find out something?"

"You could say that. Seems word got out about the battle at Shiprock. The coven networks are buzzing big time about it."

Our concerns didn't just double or triple. If more than one

coven knows, they all know. A world full of dark witches versus two defectors and our powerless cohorts—I don't like those odds at all.

I brace myself for more bad news. "Anything about Keller and Toni?"

Egan's jaw tightens. "No. If they have them, they're keeping tight-lipped about it."

What other explanation can there be?

I drift off into my own thoughts until Egan places a fresh cup of strong coffee in front of me. "Thanks."

"Have you ever reacted to anything like you did that crypt?" Rule asks.

I shake my head. "That's what tells me it's important."

"We should go blast the thing open, see what's inside," Egan says.

"That won't work," I say.

"How do you know that?"

"Instinct. There's no visible way to open it, and if we try to force it, I have no doubt things will go very badly."

"Great. I needed one more piece of crappy news today."

"Maybe it would just react to you two that way," Rule says. "I could try."

"Unless you're hiding some superhuman strength, sounds like that's not an option either," Egan says.

I take a shaky sip of my coffee then set it on the small kitchen table. "I didn't see anything that looked even remotely like a way to get in."

"If it recognized you as a threat, maybe it would recognize I'm not one," Rule says.

I shake my head. "It can't be that simple. If anyone could touch it and have it open, surely someone would have stumbled upon that before now." While I appreciate Rule's willingness to help to the best of his abilities, I'm developing a protective instinct toward him the same as I did for Toni and Keller. Not that I'm going to come right out and say that. I've already wounded his pride once today by telling his grandmother I wouldn't put him in harm's way. But I might have unknowingly done exactly that.

Suddenly exhausted, I prop my head against my hand.

"You need to get some rest," Rule says. "Tomorrow is soon enough to figure this out."

I want to argue that it isn't soon enough, that every minute we waste is a minute that Keller and Toni might not have. But what I can't argue with is how absolutely drained I feel. I'm realizing that the struggle inside me is taking more and more effort, wearing me down. I'm afraid it's going to get worse before it gets better, and I have to be ready for that.

So I nod. "Maybe your mom and grandmother will have something for us to work with tomorrow."

Rule meets my eyes. "Is there anything else I can do for you?"

My heart shifts. Were it not for Keller, I wonder if I might fall for Rule. "I'm good, thanks."

Rule seems reluctant to leave, but he stands and heads for the door all the same. Using some of my last reserve of energy, I follow. When he opens the door, I take his hand in mine.

"Thank you for helping me get back here," I say. "If I ever say something mean-spirited or harsh to you—"

"I'll know it's not you talking." He squeezes my hand and offers a small smile before he leaves the cottage.

I watch as he disappears into the night. Rule Latimer is a good soul, and he deserves someone so much better than me.

"Don't get too attached," Egan says from the opposite side of the room.

I let out a slow sigh then close the door. "I won't." Getting attached only leads to heartbreak when you have to leave.

It's evident how much the previous day took out of me when I don't wake up until almost noon. As I wander out into the living area, I find Egan at work on the computer. He glances up and chuckles.

"Nice Bride of Frankenstein look you're rocking this morning."

I stick my tongue out at him. "Why didn't you wake me?"

"You needed the rest, and I didn't want you to drag me back into that awful basement."

"Answers aren't going to walk up to the front door and present themselves, you know."

He doesn't respond, so I trudge toward the coffee maker and luckily find some hot coffee still available. After pouring a cup, I lean back against the sink. "Anything new?"

He shakes his head. "No. And honestly, that's a bit odd. Usually somebody's saying something interesting."

"How do you get access to all this stuff anyway?" I lean forward and squint. "Is that a video feed of your house?"

"You don't want to know, and yes."

"So, nothing more about Keller and Toni?"

"Nothing. I even tried their cell phones and got voice mail. Granted, they just might not want to talk to me."

Or me.

To keep from sinking too far into sadness and worry about Keller and Toni, I head for the bathroom and take a long, hot shower. Though I feel better afterward, there's no denying I'm still drained.

"You want to take the day off?" Egan asks.

"No, the quicker we can crack open how to deal with everything, the happier I'll be."

The thought of finally being able to truly relax and not have to worry about anything propels me toward the herb shop as soon as Egan parks. I've gotten used to seeing customers in the shop and browsing until they leave. Then I can safely step into the back and head downstairs.

What I'm not ready for is having one of those customers face me and the sudden realization it's Keller Dawes, the boy I love but left without a word.

"Keller," I breathe. My heart thuds so fast and hard it reverberates throughout my entire body. He's safe. And standing right in front of me. "You're alive." Tears threaten, but I blink them back.

He takes a slow, deliberate step toward me, then another. I

don't move even though I want nothing more than to race into his arms and hold him close. When he comes within an arm's length of me, he stops and stares.

"Why?" It's only one word, but with it I know in the deepest part of myself how hurt he's been by my disappearance. How angry he is now though he holds it in check.

"You know why," I say.

Egan strides through the front door then and stops suddenly just inside. He curses under his breath. Keller shoots him a dark scowl.

"Good to see you're still breathing, too," Keller says, his voice rife with sarcasm.

"I could say the same about you," Egan says. "Guess we can stop trying to figure out how to get you back from the covens."

Keller's forehead creases.

"We heard you'd gone missing," I say as I resist touching Keller to make sure he's real. "We thought my family, or maybe Egan's had taken you."

"No, and you shouldn't be surprised we came after you," Keller says. "You heard us say as much."

"We?" Egan tries to hide his need to know Toni is here, too, but I feel his concern, his intense longing for her.

"Toni's around somewhere," Keller says. "We finally figured this had to be where you'd come if you were looking for answers. Come to the source, right?"

Fiona clears her throat where she stands behind the counter.

"Not here," I say and finally touch Keller to push him toward the front door.

"No, bring him in the back," Fiona says.

"He's not one of us," Egan says.

"Says you," Keller shoots back.

"Stop it, both of you," I say and urge Keller toward the doorway to the back room.

Before they can make it, the front door opens again.

"Egan!"

I recognize the voice of my best friend and turn in time to

see Toni racing toward Egan. She launches herself at him, but he steps out of the way, and Toni has to pull herself up short. My heart breaks as I feel how difficult it is for Egan to harden himself against Toni when what he wants to do is pull her into his arms.

The look on Toni's face breaks my heart even more. My friend looks as if she's had her love for Egan thrown back in her face as if it means nothing.

I know what Egan is doing, even understand, but it doesn't make it any easier to witness.

"Have you been here the whole time?" Toni asks, letting anger replace the joy at seeing Egan.

All he does is shrug.

Toni shifts her gaze to me, and I can't lie to her.

"Almost the entire time. We laid low for a while to make sure the coast was clear," I say.

"In the back," Fiona says, a bit more insistent.

"They're not staying," Egan says.

"The hell we're not," Toni says, sounding more like her cousin.

"Then I'm not staying." Egan stalks toward the door. When Toni starts to follow him, he stops and takes a menacing step toward her. He shoves his index finger toward her face. "Don't follow me. If you know what's good for you, you'll go back home."

"You don't scare me, Egan Byrne," Toni shoots back.

"I should."

"Well, you don't. And when you decide to stop being a jackass, I'm going to be here."

Toni isn't fooled. She knows exactly what Egan is trying to do, and I have no doubt that she has enough willpower to outlast him. That he will cave first. I suspect that's exactly what Egan fears as he spins on his heel and slams his way out the front door.

As Toni watches the boy she loves walk away from her yet again, she makes a sound of frustration. "Idiot." Then she turns toward me. I have the feeling Toni thinks the same thing about me.

"We did it to protect you," I say.

Toni sighs. "I know." Without being prompted, Toni pushes past me into the back room. With a deep sigh, I follow.

Keller stands with his arms crossed on the far side of the room from me. I feel as if he wouldn't be any farther away if he were back in North Carolina.

"I take it these are the two friends who were missing," Fiona says.

I nod then introduce Fiona to Keller and Toni.

"Nice to meet you both. I gather from the conversation that you two know about Egan and Jax and what we're up against."

"Yes, ma'am," Toni says.

"You're a witch, too?" Keller asks, his face still hard. He refuses to meet my eyes.

"Yes and no," Fiona says.

"It's a long story," I add.

Keller looks at me then, expectant but not welcoming. Anger flares up in me, and I wonder if it's just me or the something else I felt at the crypt yesterday. If Keller doesn't want to talk to me, why bother coming after me? He strides forward, grabs a dining chair, spins it backward and sits down. As he rests his forearms on the back of the chair, he stares right at me.

"As it happens, I have time," he says.

I take a deep breath and push the anger away. Then I begin to tell Keller and Toni about everything that has happened since we left Baker Gap, everything we've found out, how Fiona and her family are witches but have no powers, and how there were factions within the coven witches from the time they were formed, including a group who wanted to undo the change. When I finally get to the trip to the cemetery the day before and my strange reaction to the crypt, Fiona approaches me.

"Let me see your hands," she says.

I lift them, allowing Fiona to examine the fading burns on my fingertips.

"So this is why Rule needed the ointment. He said you'd

burned yourself on hot coffee."

I venture a glance at Keller to judge his reaction to my being with another guy. My heart aches to see no reaction whatsoever.

"Well, you've got two more researchers now," Toni says. "We can get through the rest of the material faster."

"No." I shake my head. "Egan might be a jerk right now, but he's right. You two need to go back home, where it's safe. Plus, your families are probably worried sick."

"Dad knows we're fine, and he's probably told Aunt Carol already," Keller says.

"They know? Then why are you both listed as missing?" I ask.

"That happened before my mom knew we'd left on our own," Toni says. "She's still freaked out about us being taken before, so she jumped to conclusions before Uncle Jacob could tell her that Keller had left a note."

"And your dad's okay with you going off on your own like this?" Fiona asks.

"I'm on my own a lot," Keller says. "I know how to take care of myself. So does Toni."

I glance at Toni, wondering how much her cousin has been teaching her lately.

Fiona doesn't seem satisfied with the answer as she looks at me. Unsure what the reaction will be, I wonder if telling her the truth is wise. But I feel I owe her that much for believing in Egan and me, for all the information she's provided us.

"Keller is a hunter," I say.

"You've got to be kidding me," Rule says.

I look toward the doorway and see him standing there, a backpack slung over one shoulder.

"Rule," I say.

He meets my eyes, and I see deep disbelief there. "The guy you've been worried about is a hunter? In what world does that make sense?"

I don't look at Keller, don't want to know what he must be thinking right now. I'll deal with that later.

"He's a good guy," I say.

"I'm sure he thinks he is." Rule closes the space between us. "Hunters have been around even longer than coven witches, so they've had a long time to build their holier-than-thou outlook."

"Keller's not like that. And somehow they didn't even know about coven witches until I met Keller and his father." More evidence that the covens are very good at covering their tracks.

Rule doesn't look convinced as he shifts his gaze to Keller. "Are you here to hurt Jax?"

Keller looks at Rule just as hard as Rule is staring at him. "No, not that it's any of your business."

"I'm not the one she ran away from," Rule says.

"That's enough." Fiona stands and places herself between the two boys. "How about some hot chocolate, everyone? It's chilly today, so we could use some warming up."

When no one else speaks up, I nod. "That sounds wonderful."

When Fiona leaves the room, the tension doesn't ease any. Feeling responsible for the entire mess, I shift my attention to Keller and Toni. "Rule is Fiona's grandson. He's been very important in helping us research."

"Once upon a time we were the ones helping you research," Toni says, hurt evident in her voice.

"I know. And I'm sorry we hurt you both. But you have to understand we've already put you in mortal danger more than once. We can't do it again. Luck has to run out at some point, and we aren't willing for it to run out when you are both in the line of fire."

Keller gestures toward where Rule stands at the edge of the room. "What about him? You don't care if he gets hurt?"

"I can take care of myself," Rule says.

"Yeah?" Keller says, sounding highly skeptical. "How many supernatural beings you fought? Do you even know how?"

That awful something inside me snaps to attention, sensing a fight and wanting to jump into the middle of it. "Stop it! Both of you." I look from one to the other as my healing fingertips began to sizzle. With all of my willpower, I shove the edginess down.

"I don't want anyone getting hurt, but Egan and I need answers and fast," I say. "Our best chance to get those answers is to work with Rule, Fiona and Adele. But I won't willingly put them in harm's way any more than I would you two. You all are perfectly capable of taking care of yourselves most of the time, but not facing coven witches. If that hurts your precious egos, I'm sorry, but it's the truth." I meet and hold Keller's gaze. "You know that. You've seen it with your own eyes."

Silence settles for several seconds before Toni slides forward in her seat. "You also know that we're not going anywhere, so you might as well put us to work," she says. "The more of us there are going through the material and keeping an eye out for anything wonky, the sooner we can find a solution and have this over with once and for all."

I want to argue, but I can't form the words. Toni's right, and I'm weak enough not to want to have to part from Keller again. He might be supremely angry with me right now, but at least I'm in the same room with him.

When Fiona returns with a tray of hot chocolate, she heads for the cupboard. "Come on, then. We've got work to do."

With some confused glances exchanged around the room, we stand and follow her downstairs.

The next couple of hours are tense and silent, but we manage to get through a lot of material.

"Listen to this," Toni says as she pulls a loose sheet of paper from a stack she's been sifting through. "'It is critical that the earth remain in balance. For every evil there must be an equal and opposite good. If new evil is born, nature will provide the potential for a counterbalance. But as evil is a choice, so must goodness be.'" She lifts her gaze from the paper. "You think that's what your being a white witch is, a counterbalance?"

"Maybe. What is that from?" I ask.

Toni closes the binder that holds the loose papers. "Looks like just random thoughts from several people from the year after the witch trials."

"Does it say who wrote that one?"

Toni searches both sides of the paper. "No. None of them do."

When we decide to call it a night, Keller is the first one up the steps like he can't get away from me fast enough. When Toni follows next, Rule grasps my arm. "Stay here," and I know he's referring to their family's home on the floor above the herb shop. "I don't like the idea of you with a hunter."

I ease my arm away from Rule. "He won't harm me. We . . . we care about each other."

"Yeah, I can tell that," he says as he stares up the stairs.

"He's upset, and I understand why. I wouldn't have done anything differently, but I do understand why what I did hurt him."

Rule looks away with a sigh. "Consider it a standing invitation."

I give him a weak smile before following in Keller and Toni's wake. When I reach the sidewalk outside the herb shop, Toni is the only one there.

"Where's Keller?" I ask.

Toni nods down the sidewalk. "He went to get the truck."

"I'm sorry, about everything."

"I know you are."

"You're not angry at me?"

Toni looks me in the eye. "Part of me still is, but not as much as I was at first."

I look toward the sound of a truck starting down the street. "Keller's different, cold."

"You hurt him bad, Jax. He's never loved anyone before like he loves you."

"What was I supposed do, stay and risk the two of you being killed? I feel like I used up all my luck that night at Shiprock."

"But you were more powerful than they were."

"What if it was just a fluke? You heard what I said earlier about my unstable power. What if I lose my grasp on it and hurt you both?"

"You wouldn't do that."

I sigh in frustration. "You can't know that for sure because I don't."

"Maybe I know you better than you know yourself."

I'm stunned just thinking about the fact that someone could possibly know me better than I know myself, that there is someone who would care that much. In that moment, I think that maybe faith and commitment on our side just might be stronger weapons than all the magic Egan and I have at our beck and call.

Keller pulls up next to us, and I realize that Toni isn't going to climb into the truck until I do. He lifts the console out of the way. With my heart hammering, I slide across the seat next to Keller. It's the closest I've been to him in so long. I swear I can feel the heat coming off of him, can definitely smell his distinctive guy scent, all earthy and manly. I want nothing more in that moment than to slide closer to him and have him wrap his arm around me, tell me that everything is okay and he forgives me.

But I'm not holding my breath on that one.

I tell him how to reach the cottage, but he doesn't come inside with Toni and me. I don't push him, but the silence is beginning to grate on my nerves, to agitate the anger inside me.

"Jax?"

I look up at the concern in Toni's voice. "What?"

"Are you struggling with it again?"

"Yeah. I know I didn't have a choice about what I did at Shiprock, but sometimes it feels like a mistake. Like I took in more power than my body can handle, and it's burning me up from the inside out. Even if it's ultimately good, it feels wrong more and more of the time."

Toni takes my hands. "You can beat this thing. I have absolute faith in you."

I glance toward the still closed front door. "I wish everyone did. I wish I did."

"Is Egan struggling?"

I shake my head. "No. He didn't directly take the power into him like I did. I think he gets agitated partly because we're connected now, and partly because this whole situation has been exhausting and frustrating, like looking for the right puzzle piece in the dark."

"How connected are you?" Toni asks.

I hesitate before answering, but I'm not willing to lie to Toni. "We can sense each other's emotions, power fluctuations, things like that."

"How . . . how does he feel about me?"

"How do you think he feels?"

"I want to believe he cares, but he does a really good job of trying to convince me otherwise. I just need to know that I'm not making a fool of myself, that it makes sense to have hope."

I squeeze Toni's hand. "He cares, but I don't know if he'll ever admit it again."

A shaky smile spreads across Toni's face. "That's all I needed to know. Thank you."

After Toni goes to bed in my bedroom, I try to stay awake to talk to Keller. But he still hasn't come inside when my eyes begin to droop. I scoot down on the couch so I can rest but where I'll wake up when he decides to come inside.

But when I wake again, it's the next morning. The first hint of daylight is peeking through the blinds, and someone has placed a blanket over me. I think it was probably Toni until I roll over and see Keller spread out on the loveseat, his long legs hanging over the end. I know in that moment that he was the one to drape the cover over me, and that no matter how angry he is he still cares about me. That knowledge does more to beat back the darkness within me than all the pushing and shoving I've done since I left Baker Gap.

I smile. If Keller still loves me, I can do anything.

Chapter Seven

Egan shows back up as Keller, Toni and I are eating breakfast. "They sure don't grow them very bright in North Carolina, do they?" he says.

"I see you're still on track for Jerk of the Year," Keller shoots back without looking up from his bowl of cereal.

"Says the idiot who has a death wish."

I stand and walk across the room. I don't say anything to anyone else as I stride out the door and slam it behind me. It's early enough that when I reach the herb shop, Rule is still there. I don't go inside despite the cold air. Instead, I sit on a metal bench next to the sidewalk.

"Hey, you're going to freeze out here," Rule says as he comes to sit beside me.

I start to speak, but it comes out strangled. Everything I've been holding inside demands to be set free. A tear rolls down my cheek.

"Hey, now," Rule says as he reaches over and wipes away the tear. "What's wrong?"

"Everything." I tell him about how messed up everything is with Egan and Toni, Keller and me. How I thought leaving Baker Gap was the right thing to do, but that it's just made a mess of everything.

"You take too much on yourself." He turns my face toward him, lifts my chin. "Even someone as powerful as you can only take so much."

His eyes really are pretty, different shades of brown and green dancing together. For a moment I get lost in them, wishing everything in my life could be different, simpler. That moment is all he needs to lower his lips to mine. The contact is warm, soft, and for just a moment I allow myself to kiss him back. But it's wrong when my heart belongs to someone else, even if that someone will barely speak to me.

I pull away. "No, I can't."

"Jax," he whispers against my wet lips.

"She said no." Keller jerks Rule away and shoves him against a nearby tree.

I thought I'd seen him angry before, but it was nothing compared to the fire burning in his eyes now. I gasp when the darkness inside me takes notice. "No," I say.

Rule pushes away from the tree and looks like he might throw a punch at Keller. Not that Keller seems to mind. He's poised to throw one right back, and he has a lot more practice at fighting.

"Come on guys, cut it out," Toni says as she comes running up the sidewalk.

My head begins to pound. "No!" I scream. The hairs stand up on my arms, and the air crackles. "Just stop it." I'm vaguely aware of my friends saying my name, but it's as if I'm listening through cotton stuffed in my ears. My ponytail starts to lift away from my neck.

Keller grabs my hand, and everything goes back to normal in an instant. It happens so quickly that I stagger and nearly fall onto the bench.

I feel my eyes widen in surprise as I look at Keller. What just happened? It's like his touch flipped an off switch in me.

I notice two women across the street staring and wonder just how much I've shown of who I really am. "I've got to get out of here."

Keller doesn't let go of my hand, trying to keep me from leaving. "Jax."

I nearly start crying at the sound of my name on his lips. Why couldn't he have said it last night when I didn't feel like a giant spotlight was burning into the top of my head?

Of course I'm stronger than him and free myself easily. I hurry away from them all, but it's not until I'm out of sight of the curious women and my friends that I begin to run.

The sun is at its zenith when someone finally shows up at the cemetery where I've been sitting all morning after running away from my friends. I haven't approached the crypt or tried to touch it. Instead, I simply sit on a cracked stone bench at the edge of the cemetery and stare at the crypt, asking myself a stream of questions about it.

When Keller enters through the gate, I take a deep breath not knowing what to expect. I sense he's much calmer than he was earlier. That's a start.

"Is it okay if I sit down?" he asks.

I nod without looking up at him. The last thing I need today is to add becoming a blubbering idiot to kissing Rule and nearly showing my power in public. While I've thought about all that while sitting here, what has really occupied my mind is how Keller's touch calmed it all, like it had in my dream.

When he sits close, he makes me jittery and calms me at the same time just as he has ever since I met him. It doesn't make any sense, and I doubt I can explain it to anyone, but he alone has that effect on me.

"I'm sorry about earlier," he says.

"The ignoring me or the stupid fight with Rule?"

"Both." He goes silent for several seconds. "Are you two a couple now?"

"No."

"I guess it would make more sense than the two of us. Even if he has no powers, he's still a witch."

I take a risk and wrap my hand around Keller's. "Listen to me. Rule is just a friend. Yes, he'd like to be more, but that's not what I want."

Our eyes meet. "What do you want?" Keller asks.

"Something I can't have, at least not now."

He lifts his hand to my cheek and strokes it gently. I close my eyes and focus solely on the feel of his touch.

"Why can't you?" he asks.

I sigh and open my eyes. Reluctantly, I pull away from his touch and release his hand. "It's still too dangerous for you to be around me. Actually, it's more dangerous now than when I left

Baker Gap."

"Because of your increased power?"

"Yes. It frightens me that I don't fully understand it, that I might not be able to handle it." I swallow hard. "I'm scared that I'll end up hurting someone when that's the thing I'm trying to prevent."

"You're too strong for that to happen."

"I'd like to think so, but there's so much I don't understand. What I don't know is scarier than what I do."

"It seems to me that I can help you with it."

I glance at him and know he's referring to when he'd touched me earlier, and the struggle inside me died, at least temporarily.

"Has that happened before when anyone else has touched you?" he asks. "Rule?"

"No. But there's no guarantee that it'll happen again."

"But we can test it if it does. It's important, I feel it. Think about it. If I'm there, you could access your full power without worrying about it getting out of control. This might be the thing that helps us defeat the covens."

"One witch and one hunter against hundreds of dark witches?"

"One other witch, two hunters, three sort-of witches, and you, more powerful than all the rest of us combined."

I let out a long breath and look away, focusing on one of the headstones worn away by time and weather. I wish I could find a way to fix everything without putting anyone I care about in danger, but I just don't know if that's possible.

"Are you fighting that darkness right now?" Keller asks.

I realize I'm not and shake my head. "It calmed the moment you slid onto the bench beside me." I remember the text about balance that Toni found and wonder if Keller's calming effect on me plays into that somehow. "But I don't want to depend on you for this, not when it puts you in danger of being killed. I need to learn to control this myself."

"You are so stubborn." Keller stands suddenly and stalks several steps away before turning to face me. "I may not be a witch, but I'm not helpless either. This calming effect I have on your dark magic, maybe that's supposed to be my contribution to this fight. And you're not going to keep me from it, even if you don't want to be with me anymore."

"It's not that I don't want to be with you."

He holds up a hand. "I know, you think you can't. Or so you say."

"What does that mean?"

He lowers his hand. "You did kiss Rule."

"He kissed me."

"But you didn't stop him."

"I did. I was pushing away when you jerked him up. You know that."

"For a moment, Jax, you did kiss him. I saw that, too."

The darkness wakes again, starts churning. "I was upset, okay? Lonely."

Keller walks toward me, starts to reach for my hand. I'm so upset that I jerk away from him. "What are you doing?"

"Your dark magic is near the surface now," he says. "We need to test the theory, make sure the calming effect I have on you wasn't a one-time thing."

I want to tell him to leave me alone, to punish him for hurting me. But that's selfish. Taking care of the covens trumps my personal feelings. Reluctantly, I nod.

Keller takes both of my hands in his. At first, I think it doesn't work, but then I realize that what I'm still feeling isn't my magic. It's just hurt feelings and guilt, normal stuff.

"Did it work?" he asks.

I nod. A bit of the agitation resurfaces when he drops my hands, but nothing near the level it was before.

Keller takes a few steps away. "Good to know." He sounds so distant that it breaks my heart.

I don't know if it will do any good or if it's even wise to clear the air, but I have to. "Rule has been a good friend, and you've been ignoring me. Why'd you even come here if you can't stand to be near me?"

"Can't stand to . . . ? Are you crazy? It's all I can do to not pull you into my arms and kiss you senseless."

"You have a funny way of showing it."

Keller moves fast for a person with no supernatural powers. Before I can speak, he crosses the distance between us and pulls me off the bench into his arms.

"This is how much I've missed you." His lips take mine, and it's not a soft, tender kiss like Rule gave me this morning.

I melt against Keller. I run my hands up his back, feeling the wonderful definition of his muscles. Not the beefy kind sported by weight junkies but lean, powerful muscles born of hunting dangerous supernatural creatures. I realize that even without the covens, I could lose him. That fear makes me kiss him even deeper, longer, barely breathing.

Keller lifts me off my feet and holds me so close I can feel his heart beating wildly against mine. I lose track of how long we kiss as I hang on to him and make up for lost time. It feels as if we've been apart a year instead of mere weeks.

When we come up for air, Keller frames my face with his hands and looks deeply into my eyes. "Did that feel like I don't care?"

"No." My answer comes out a whisper. "But I maybe could use a bit more convincing."

Keller's lips stretch into a smile, and my heart fills with love. He's about to lower his lips to mine again when the sound of an approaching vehicle stops him. When he takes a couple of steps away from me, I suddenly feel how cold the air has grown. Or maybe it's been like that all day, and being with Keller has simply caused my body to heat up.

"We should go," Keller says. He takes my hand in his and starts for the gate.

A jolt of surprise goes through me when I notice who is getting out of the car.

"What is it?" Keller asks.

I don't have time to answer before Sarah the librarian and another woman are within earshot.

"Well, hello," Sarah says when she sees us. "Still doing research?"

"Yeah. Nobody in my family here though." I squeeze Keller's hand slightly, hoping he understands not to say anything revealing. "Though this is an interesting old cemetery."

"It is, isn't it? This is my good friend, Amanda. We come out here a few times a year to clean the place up. It's sad when these old cemeteries are lost because all the descendants have died off or moved away."

What Sarah says sounds totally plausible, but my intuition insists Sarah isn't exactly telling the whole truth. But to what end?

I let my power reach out a bit and examine Sarah again, but still there's no indication she's anything other than a librarian. Perhaps an overly curious librarian, but a librarian nonetheless.

"So none of these people have relatives living here anymore?" I ask.

"It's possible they do, but they don't get out here to clean. Maybe they're too old."

"Do you even know who some of these graves belong to?" I ask. "Some of the stones don't have names."

"I've tried to come up with names over the years, and I've found a few," Sarah says. "But some of their identities have been lost to time, unfortunately."

"I think it's one of the saddest things, leaving no record of your existence behind," Amanda says.

My thoughts go to all those harmless witches who were killed during the witch hunts, all those people, whole families lost to history. But there are names that weren't lost.

I nod. "At least some of them have clues. Like the crypt back there." I point toward the imposing stone structure. "It's so different than any other grave here. All I saw was a last name, Davenport, and that ornate sun on the front. They must have been a wealthy family to have such a nice crypt."

Sarah hesitates for a touch too long. I doubt anyone else would have noticed. "I believe they were," she says. "Though we don't know much about them. They left the area in the late 1600s, I believe."

"So not long after the witch trials?" I say. "Were they

caught up in the hysteria?"

"I think most people were, one way or another."

How's that for a non-answer? Time for a more direct question. "Do you know who's interred in the crypt?"

Sarah meets my gaze, and I get the sense she's searching for something. "Penelope Davenport."

I do my best not to react. "Who was she?"

"The daughter of a wealthy ship builder."

"Reginald Davenport?"

Sarah can't hide her surprise at my question. "Yes. Where did you come across that name?"

I shrug. "Not sure. I've looked at so many dusty old records lately."

"And his name stuck out?" There's definite suspicion in her question, and the darkness within me rises from its temporary slumber.

Keller squeezes my hand, calming me.

"Yeah. He sounds like a guy with loads of money, doesn't he? All stuffy and proper. Hard to believe someone like that could have gotten caught up in all the craziness of the witch trials."

"It didn't matter if you were rich or poor, man or woman, well respected or not," Amanda says.

"All that had to happen was for someone point the finger at you." Sarah points her finger at me, and the hairs on my arms stand on end.

"Glad things aren't like that now," Keller says, and I think I hear a note of subtle warning in his voice. Then he tugs on my hand. "We better get going."

I want to stay and dig for more answers, but something tells me to trust him. After all, we're walking away with more information that we had when we arrived.

"Okay. It was nice to see you again," Sarah says to me. "Come to the library any time you need help with research."

Once we're in Keller's truck, he glances at me. "Thanks for trusting me."

"Why did you pull me away?"

"As soon as she got near us, I felt a vibration start in you. It kept getting stronger the longer you talked to her. I figured we better leave before we had another incident like this morning."

I glance out the windshield, but Sarah and Amanda have disappeared into the back of the cemetery. "I can't put my finger on it, but I've felt like she's been watching me since I got to Salem."

"Is she a witch?"

I shake my head. "I don't detect a signature."

"Could she be like Fiona's family?"

I notice he doesn't mention Rule by name. "I don't think so. Even with them, there's the slightest disturbance in the air around them. Sarah just feels . . . odd but normal, if that makes any sense. When I was at the Pherson property, I felt a faint echo of a witch watching us, but it wasn't like when I've been face to face with Sarah."

"You think it's possible she's part of the Bane?"

I stare toward the cemetery for several seconds before answering. "Anything's possible, but if so, she's found some way to completely cloak the fact that she's a witch."

"That would be useful to know, especially if you and Egan could use the same method to hide yourselves from the covens."

"I can't figure her out. She seems friendly, always offering to help me, but I sense curiosity and a bit of suspicion coming from her, too."

"We'll see what we can find out about her and her friend." He starts the engine and heads back toward town.

"Could they be hunters? How can you even tell if someone's a hunter?"

"It's one of those 'takes one to know one' things. There's a certain glint in the eyes, especially among the hunters who have been doing it for a long time. They're always wary but pretty good at not letting it show to anyone who isn't watching for it."

Keller squeezes the steering wheel until his knuckles go white before relaxing his grasp. "These two didn't seem like hunters, but I'll ask my dad if he knows of any hunters in this area."

"You're in contact with him?"

"I haven't been since we left, but he might have information we need. If Sarah and Amanda are hunters, or even if there are other hunters here, we need to know that."

I don't like the idea of Keller contacting Rev. Dawes, afraid the man might decide the greater good of ridding the world of supernatural threat is more important than making sure he doesn't lose his son. But Keller has handled his father before, so I have to trust him.

As I watch the world zip by outside my window, I think about Sarah's appearance at the cemetery, the same out-of-the-way cemetery where Penelope Davenport is buried. "The more I think about it, the more I think it's possible Sarah and maybe Amanda are members of the Bane. It would explain why I've had that feeling of being watched since I arrived in Salem. They'd know I'm a witch."

"Did you sense a threat from either of them?"

"No, not exactly. Wariness, but no overt hostility. Part of me just wants to march up and ask her if she's part of the Bane."

"Maybe that's what you do eventually, but I think we need to try to learn a little more first. The last thing we need is to make another enemy."

"True. I've got those coming out my ears."

When we return to the cottage, Rule's car is parked at the curb. As we walk up the path to the cottage, Keller wraps my hand in his as if to lay claim.

"You have nothing to worry about," I say softly.

"Just a little insurance that he doesn't go stealing kisses again."

I roll my eyes then tug on Keller's hand until he stops walking. "Listen. This morning was a mistake, but Rule is a good friend. He and his family have helped us a lot. And we still need to work together, at least until Egan and I feel it's too dangerous for them."

I'm not about to tell Keller, but Egan and I will find a way to protect him and Toni, too, even if it means hurting their feelings again. Bruised feelings can be fixed. Being killed can't.

"Fine, but I don't have to like the guy," he says.

"No, you don't. But I think eventually you will."

He gives me a half-grin. "You have way too much faith in me."

When we walk inside, Rule and Toni are watching TV and eating from a big bowl of popcorn.

"Did I forget it was movie day or something?" I ask.

"Don't particularly feel like working at the moment," Toni says. She doesn't have to look in Egan's direction for me to know that he probably said something insensitive.

"Well, some of us are still working," Egan says under his breath.

I give him a hard stare. He shrugs and goes back to staring at his computer screen.

Rule stands and sizes up Keller, probably trying to figure out if Keller is going to toss him out on his head. Rule isn't a weak guy, but Keller stands a few inches taller and wider. And he's already fought more fights than Rule likely will during his entire life.

I walk farther into the room and prop my hip against the end of the couch. "So, we have news."

"The covens have suddenly fallen off the face of the earth?" Egan says, sarcastically hopeful.

"Sadly, no. But we did find Penelope Davenport. She's the resident of that crypt that's spelled."

"How'd you find that out?" Rule asks.

"Ran into Sarah the local librarian and her friend there. They confirmed that it's Penelope. Oh, and we think they might be members of the Bane." I give the rundown of the entire conversation.

"So what now?" Toni asks.

"We see if we can find any more information about the Bane. If not, I go with the direct approach and ask her if she's a witch and a member of the Bane. I'd rather go in armed with more knowledge, though, so I'm not caught off guard by anything."

"We can go all hands on deck with the research tomorrow,"

Toni says.

A lull in the conversation starts getting uncomfortable with Keller and Rule in the same room and Toni and Egan still barely speaking to each other.

"Jax, can I talk to you?" Rule asks, breaking the silence.

Keller's hand tightens on mine, but I slip free and give him a look that tells him to behave.

"Sure." I nod toward the front door, and Rule follows me outside to a gazebo that sits at the back corner of the cottage. It reminds me of the one in Toni's back yard, though the vines on this one have slipped into their winter nap.

"I want to apologize for what happened this morning," he says.

"It was partly my fault."

"But I knew you still cared for him. I can't say anything other than kissing you was selfish on my part. I wanted to, and I did it."

"I'm not sure this helps at all, but it was a nice kiss."

Rule laughs a little. "Not really."

"I'm sorry. You are a great guy, a great catch."

He starts to speak.

I hold up my hand. "Wait, let me finish." I take a step closer to him, and if Keller is looking he'll just have to deal with it. "I can honestly say that were it not for the fact that I love Keller, things might be different between you and me. I know that probably doesn't make you feel any better, but I wanted you to know the truth. Someone will be lucky to have you someday."

He looks at me with a touch of sadness. "Maybe."

"Why don't you sound like you believe me?"

"Think about it. When will I ever meet anyone else with whom I can share my family's secret?"

I hadn't thought of it that way, and I scramble for something to say. "I never thought I'd find anyone to share my secrets with either, but I did. And in the most unexpected place."

Rule glances at the cottage. "How does that work anyway?"

"Keller isn't like other hunters. I mean, he's good at what he does, but he's not blind to shades of gray. At least not anymore."

"Seems like everything we've ever believed is being turned on its head."

"You can say that again."

"Seems like everything—" Before he can finish repeating himself, I punch him playfully in the arm. Rule laughs. "We should go back inside before hunter boy decides he needs to hunt me."

I grab Rule's hand and hold it between mine. "Seriously, Rule, thank you for everything. When I left my coven, I wanted a normal life with normal friends. But there was this part of me that didn't really believe it would happen."

"Well, if you look around we're not really all that normal. You've got a hunter, a girl with pink in her hair who has the serious hots for a witch, and a witch with no powers."

I smile at him. "Sounds like the perfect friends to me."

"Everyone's great, yada, yada, yada," Egan says as he appears suddenly on the path to the cottage. "Come inside so I only have to say this once."

Worry spikes in me as I follow Egan inside, Rule close on my heels. "What's wrong?"

"I've been watching the online chatter in the hunter community the past several days, and today when I checked my normal sources there's nothing. It's gone stone cold quiet."

"That's good, right?" Rule asks. "You don't want hunters after you." He glances at Keller like there's a part of him that still didn't trust Keller.

"No, it's not good. It means something's up," Egan says.

"They know you're watching them," Toni says.

Egan doesn't even look at her. "They at least suspect they might be watched, so they're not taking chances."

"You think this means they know where we are?" I ask.

"We'll know soon enough. Which means all of you need to clear out of here." He points at Keller and Rule and makes a vague gesture in Toni's direction.

"You know, that line's getting mighty damned old," Toni says as she stands.

Egan's anger flares as he spins toward Toni. "Well, I'm

going to keep saying it until it sinks into that thick skull of yours."

Instead of making her angry, his words make Toni smile. I know what Toni's thinking, that if Egan didn't care about her he wouldn't be pushing so hard for her to leave for a safer locale.

"You two have to accept that we're not going anywhere," Keller says. He glances at Rule. "Neither is Rule, evidently. And I think we've proven that we can find you if you pull a Houdini again. So let's just accept we're all here for the long haul and figure out what we're going to do to prepare."

"Well, you can call your pops and ask him what the hell is going on," Egan says.

"Since you asked so nicely."

Egan flips Keller the bird as Keller reaches for his new cell phone.

"Classy." Phone in hand, Keller heads to Egan's bedroom and shuts the door.

Rule sinks onto the couch next to Toni where he'd been sitting when Keller and I returned from the cemetery. Egan's jaw goes rigid, but instead of saying something he stalks into the kitchen and grabs a Dr. Pepper from the fridge.

I follow him. "Careful. You clench your jaw any harder, and you'll break your perfect teeth."

He shoots me an annoyed look then glances toward the living room. "What, Rule figured out he can't have you so he's moving on to the next girl he sees?"

"What do you care? You obviously don't want her anymore."

Egan growls under his breath. "Don't be stupid."

This time, it's my anger that flares to life. "Don't be an ass."

He doesn't look comfortable talking honestly about his feelings, but they spill out anyway. "You know how hard this is for me."

"Because you love her."

"Yes, damn it. Because I love her."

"You know she's not going to leave. You might as well give in."

"I can't."

"Why?"

"Because if she dies I won't be able to handle it," he says, pain written across his face. "I'll lose my grip on anything good in myself."

"You don't know that."

He meets my eyes with a look so intense it shakes me all the way through. "I do. Can you stand there and tell me the same thing wouldn't happen to you if Keller were killed?"

The very thought makes my heart squeeze with a pain so real it causes me to gasp.

"That's what I thought." Without another word, Egan stalks out the back door.

For a long time, I just stare at the space where he'd stood, wondering if he's right. If I lose Keller, will I go so dark that even my coven will pale in comparison?

Chapter Eight

Footsteps approach the kitchen. By their weight on the floor, I know it's not one of the guys. When I finally turn around, Toni is standing at the entrance to the room. Her normally messy-styled hair lies flat, and the pink streak is fading away.

"He's not going to change his mind, is he?" she asks.

I don't have the heart to lie to Toni. "I'd like to think he will, but I honestly don't know."

Toni looks so deflated, so different from how she looked earlier, that I want to take her in my arms and promise everything will work out. Only I can't promise that, not when I'm not even sure if any of us will survive another month, another week, another day.

"Part of me thinks I should have listened to you back when you warned me about him when we met, but there's a much bigger part that isn't sorry about one moment I've spent with Egan," Toni says. "Even if he never says a nice word to me again."

"Oh, Toni."

"No, that's not me being pathetic. I'm just grateful that I've known what that feels like, being crazy in love." She says it as if she'll never experience that feeling again, and that makes me so angry that I want to hunt Egan down and smack some sense into him.

Yes, being around Toni and Keller puts them in danger. But Keller also seems to help me keep a grip on my new power. And don't we all deserve a moment of pure happiness if our time is short?

Before I try to figure out what to say, how to make everything better, Toni gives me a sad smile and walks away.

I wait in the kitchen a couple more minutes, feeling like the literal weight of the world is sitting on my shoulders. When I finally wander into the living room, Keller is just coming out of the bedroom.

"Did you reach your dad?" I ask.

He nods, and from the tight look on his face, it wasn't a pleasant conversation. "Where's Egan?"

"As far away from me as possible," Toni says as she shoves more popcorn in her mouth.

Keller's hands tighten into fists.

I catch his gaze and shake my head. He doesn't look happy about it, but he lets the topic drop.

"Dad says he thinks something big is up, but he doesn't know what. Seems word has gotten around that his son is friendly with witches."

"He's been cut out?" I ask.

"Some places. He still has some feelers out with a couple of his long-time hunting buddies. He says he'll let me know if he finds out anything."

"What about the other issue?"

"What other issue?" Toni asks.

"Sarah and Amanda aren't hunters, at least not to my dad's knowledge," Keller says.

Rule turns in his seat, his eyes wider than normal. "Sarah Davenport."

"What?" I ask.

"I just remembered, her last name is Davenport."

We all stare stunned for several moments.

"A fact she neglected to mention," Keller says.

"I think we just got our answer about whether she's a member of the Bane."

Now I just have to figure out exactly what I'm going to do about it.

When I emerge from my bedroom before dawn the next morning after having a nightmare about that night at Shiprock, one in which I didn't defeat my coven, I find Egan at the kitchen table drinking coffee and eating a huge bear claw. "Caffeine and copious amounts of sugar. I see you're starting your day off healthy."

He lifts his half-eaten pastry. "Breakfast of champions."

I roll my eyes then cross to the sink and pour myself a glass of water. "So, you here to stay now, or are you going to pull another disappearing act as soon as Toni gets up?"

He tosses down his bear claw. "We have so many bigger things to worry about. Why are you on my case about this?"

"Because you're hurting her."

"Good. Maybe she'll leave."

I take a long drink of water then start a pot of coffee to give myself time to come up with something to say that doesn't sound bitchy. "I don't think so. She's stubborn, and tougher than you know."

"And I can be a real ass. Trust me, she'll leave at some point."

I turn toward Egan. "Is that really what you want?"

He meets my eyes. "Yes."

I see that part of him believes this, but he also can no longer hide his feelings from me. There is longing there, desire, heartache. I don't miss the brief glance he spares the bedroom door behind which Toni still sleeps.

"Then you should leave," I say.

He jerks his gaze back to me. "You want to go?"

"Not me. You."

"Well, that's just stupid. Our odds of surviving together are pretty low, so you by yourself would be virtually nonexistent."

I lift and wiggle my fingers. "I'm a big, bad white witch, remember?"

"Even if you are, you're about as stable as a war-torn country."

I place my hands on my hips. "You're right, you can be an ass."

"It's the truth, and you know it," he says, not backing down.

"And I've found a way to control my new power levels."

"How?"

"Keller. For some reason, when my dark magic starts bubbling to the surface, he can touch me, and it calms."

"So, what, he's the witch whisperer now?"

"I don't know why or how it works, but it does. And as much as I want to keep him safe, this might be the key to everything. If I can access my full magical potential without worrying about losing control, I have to consider having him be right in the thick of things." I catch Egan's gaze and hold it. "Toni might be able to do the same for you."

"No."

"Don't dismiss it without even thinking about it."

Egan shoves to his feet and walks several steps away from me. "This isn't your decision to make." He shakes his head. "And I can't believe after we left Baker Gap to protect them that you suddenly want to put them on the front lines of whatever crapstorm is heading our way."

"I don't want to, but I may end up doing a lot of things I don't want to so that we can get rid of the coven threat."

He shakes his head again, looking disgusted.

"What if we're more powerful together than apart?"

"Do you really think that could possibly be true?"

"Maybe."

The far bedroom door opens before we come to any sort of agreement. Keller steps out in just a pair of jeans, his chest bare. Despite the seriousness of our current situation and my tense conversation with Egan, my heart rate accelerates at the sight.

"Everything okay out here?" Keller asks as he walks toward us.

"We were just discussing whether or not Egan should leave if he's going to continue to treat Toni like he doesn't care."

"That's not all we were discussing," Egan says, irritated.

"Toni would do it, you know," Keller says, letting us know he'd heard our conversation. "If you stick around."

Egan throws up his hands. "I'm not going anywhere, not until this is all over." He glances up at me then Keller. "And evidently no one else is either. Can't say that makes us the brightest bunch ever to walk the earth."

I sense a lessening of Egan's resistance, and it gives me hope. But as I look at Keller, and a wave of love for him hits me, I wonder if I'm making a mistake. Maybe Egan is the smarter of us to want to protect those we love at all cost, even our own heartache and loneliness. I hate feeling pulled in two directions.

I shake my head, trying to clear the doubts. I have to play this one day at a time, one strategic decision at a time based on what little information I have. I want to think that if and when things become too dangerous for Keller, Toni and even Rule and his family that I can make the tough decision to leave them again, even if it makes them hate me. But I know it may not be that simple this time. My stomach knots at the thought that I may have to put Keller in mortal danger so that I can do what is necessary to save the world from the covens' wrath.

Toni trudges out of the bedroom in her pajama pants and a *Battlestar Galactica* T-shirt that has "So say we all" written across the front. It's a departure from her Whedon collection, but somehow it fits this morning. We need to stop arguing and avoiding each other and work together. I worry though as Toni heads for the coffeepot without a word, her hair sticking out in all directions. She hasn't even tried to look nice before Egan sees her.

Oddly enough I sense a well of affection rise up in him as he watches her. It's the first time since Keller and Toni's arrival in Salem that she's ignored him, and he hasn't been able to take his eyes off her.

No one says anything until Toni pours herself a cup of coffee and takes a seat at the table opposite where Egan is standing. When she finally looks up, she's all business. Her lack of normal Toni pep breaks my heart, but maybe the stress of not knowing what the covens are doing or when they might show up here has changed us all. As I think about it, I realize it's true. We're all different, harder than we were only a few short weeks ago when we became a foursome.

"So, what's the plan of attack for today?" Toni asks.

Everyone looks at me, and in that moment I actually feel like a leader. "Divide and conquer," I say. "Toni, I'd like you to help Rule and his family continue researching. We need the names of those other girls who disappeared after the trials, any other information you can find about the Bane. Egan, find out everything you can about the Davenport family in this area."

"What about you?" Egan asks.

"Surveillance. Before I confront Sarah, I want to watch what she does and where she goes. Maybe it will lead us to some answers, like if there are other Bane members, and if we can trust them."

"I'll go with you," Keller says. "It's what I do—track, observe, and eliminate threats if necessary."

Is it wrong that I find him really hot right now?

Egan looks from Keller to Toni and back. "There's really no chance of us getting you two to steer clear of this mess?"

"Nope," Toni says.

Keller leans back in his chair. "Even if I didn't have this strange ability to temper Jax's power, I'd still stay. You're not the only ones who need to be a part of this fight. It's not just your lives that are affected by the covens. Every single person in the world is in danger if they're not stopped. Have been for hundreds of years. You can either let us work with you, really work with you, or we're going to work on it on our own."

Egan makes a disgusted sound, but I keep staring at Keller. It hits me, right in my center, that he's right. How would I feel if I put my fate in someone else's hands, someone I loved, and let him take all the risk while I stayed hidden in relative safety? I lived too long with my destiny in the hands of others, and it was stifling. How can I ask Keller, Toni, anyone to do the same?

"You're right," I say. I don't know if I'll feel the same way if Keller's in true danger, but for now I'm going to try to respect his wish to have a hand in his own destiny.

Egan sighs.

"They have the right to make their own decisions," I say.

"Even if those decisions get them killed."

"Yes. Are we any different? We could die same as them. In fact, the covens are more likely to kill us than people who can do them no harm." I know Keller would like to argue that point, about him not being able to make a dent in the covens' armor, but he doesn't say so now.

Egan paces toward the front door then back. "If we're preparing for a real battle, everyone needs training. Serious training."

"I agree," Keller says. "It just so happens, I came prepared."

For the first time in what seems like forever, I see Egan smile. "Take some of Papa Dawes' arsenal?"

"Nope. Brought my own."

Egan laughs. "Now we're talking."

By the time Keller and I head out to watch Sarah's movements, Egan has provided us with some background information including her address and the fact that she's not married and has no children.

"Not exactly a good way to keep the family line going," I say as we walk toward Keller's truck.

"I'm guessing there's not an online dating site for witches." Keller's words are so like Rule's that I realize all over again how lucky I am to have found Keller.

As I climb into the passenger side of his truck, I try not to think about ever losing him.

Keller slides into his seat and slips the key into the ignition. He starts the truck and puts it into gear. He drives out of town past Pioneer Village, a historical site that sits on the opposite side of the harbor from downtown Salem. About a mile before we reach Marblehead, he turns down a street on the right. A few houses down, he slows and points out my side of the truck. "That's Sarah's house."

I look out across a small lawn toward a little white clapboard house, the type of house a librarian might live in.

Keller eases by as the front door opens and Sarah heads out to her car with a thermal mug, purse and book bag. When she looks toward the street, I lean back in my seat so she hopefully doesn't recognize me. Keller stays calm and drives on by at a normal speed and makes a right at the next street.

For the next several minutes, we follow at a distance as Sarah drops mail into the box outside the post office, goes through the fast food drive-through for a breakfast sandwich, and finally heads for the library. Since the library isn't yet open, Keller and I go back to the restaurant and drive through for our own breakfast. We park at the end of the block that holds the library.

"Well, she seems perfectly boring so far," he says between bites.

"Looks can be deceiving."

My phone rings so I pull my gaze away from the library to answer the call from Egan. "You have something new?"

"Yeah. I found several Davenports in the earliest records for the area, including Reginald, but the references stop shortly after the witch trials," he says. "They don't show up again until about fifty years ago."

If Sarah is related to Reginald and Penelope, where had her family gone during all those intervening years? And why did they come back?

"I also ran over to the herb shop to look at all those old property maps again. You know, the real ones. I didn't catch it at first because they're not on the same map, but it turns out good old Reginald Davenport owned the property behind the Phersons. Don't know if that helps at all, but thought I'd mention it."

"Thanks." When I hang up, I share the information with Keller.

"The plot thickens."

So we don't look so obvious about basically stalking Sarah, Keller and I wait until the library has been open about half an hour before we go in. She's at the front desk when we walk through the entrance.

"Good morning," she says and smiles. "Here to take me up on my offer of help?"

"Maybe." I step close to the counter. "I'm really intrigued by that crypt we saw at the cemetery the other day. Thought it would be interesting to learn more about this Penelope Davenport and her family."

"Have you found a connection to your family?"

"As a matter of fact, I have. Turns out Reginald Davenport and my ancestors were neighbors."

Sarah tries to hide her shock but doesn't quite succeed. I imagine her mind racing, trying to figure out how I could have possibly figured that out based on the faulty maps upstairs.

"Always interesting when you find another piece of the puzzle," she finally says as she reaches for a book on the countertop.

I notice a silver bracelet on her wrist, one adorned with several swirls of raised silver against a smooth background. It's hard to tell, but it seems to have a double spiral at its center. The sight of it shakes me because it's similar to the design on a belt buckle and earrings my mother gave me for my last birthday before she died. "That's a pretty bracelet," I say.

Sarah tries to be sly about it, but she casually shifts so that the cuff of her blouse covers the bracelet. "Thank you." She takes a step back. "If you'll excuse me, I have to go lead storytime."

I wait until she's left for the children's room before I turn to Keller. "Think I hit a nerve?"

Though we've already gone through all the material in the history room, we head upstairs for appearances' sake. Once we're behind the closed door, we use the time to do check-ins. I text Toni to see if she's found any new information in the basement o' documents, and Keller checks in with his dad. We both come away empty-handed.

"What was with the comment about Sarah's bracelet?" Keller asks.

"Maybe it's nothing, but I have a belt buckle and earrings with the same symbol, ones my mother gave me."

"Do you know what it means?"

I shake my head. "I always thought it was just pretty. And maybe that's all it is. Sometimes I feel like I'm reading too much into every little thing that I would otherwise chalk up to a coincidence."

"Sometimes it's hard to tell the difference."

We spend a half-hour sifting through materials in the room just in case something new miraculously pops up and says, "Hey, I'm important." What I want to do is just walk up to Sarah and stop beating around the bush. But the middle of the public library doesn't seem like the best place to confront someone who may be another witch about her identity.

I push away from the table. "Let's go."

But when we reach the first floor, Sarah is nowhere to be seen. Storytime is over, and she's not behind the checkout counter or in the stacks.

I head for the front door. As I expected, her car is gone. "Crap."

"Come on," Keller says as he grabs my hand. "Salem isn't that big. She's got to be around somewhere."

But after driving through the main part of Salem, past her house, down what feels like every street in town, and passing by the library again in case she's come back, it feels more like she's gone up in a puff of smoke.

After grabbing a couple of to-go coffees, we head for the Wildwood Cemetery on the off chance Sarah has gone to the crypt. But the place is empty except for the long departed.

"Well, I don't think the CIA is going to be tapping us to be spies anytime soon," I say.

"She'll turn up."

"Not if we've spooked her." Damn it, why hadn't I just confronted her at the library and depended on Keller to keep me calm should the need arise?

By the time we roll back into Salem, it's lunchtime so we stop at a burger place on the edge of town. We get our food to go so we can head over to the herb shop. But when we come outside, Sarah steps into our path as we approach the truck.

"Why are you following me?" she asks, all hints of her former friendly demeanor gone.

"I could ask you the same question, Miss Davenport. Along with a ton of others, like why you broke into our cottage."

Sarah doesn't respond, and we're set to have a stare-down until I decide to cut to the chase. "I know you're a witch and probably a member of the Bane."

"How can you possibly know that?" Sarah doesn't even try to deny it now. The time for that is past.

"That's not important. What is important is the fact that I need to know if the Bane really exist and if they can help me."

"A dark coven witch wants help? Doing what, destroying mankind? You are doing a pretty good job of that without our help."

The darkness inside me surges to the surface, stronger than before. Keller must notice it because he places his palm against my back. Despite his touch, it takes longer than the other times for the darkness to recede. I notice that it doesn't completely go away and try not to think it's growing in strength.

"Do you honestly think that if that's why I was trying to find you that you'd still be alive right now?"

Sarah narrows her eyes. "Why else would you seek us out?"

I take a deep breath, trying to calm myself against her barrage of doubt and accusation. "Because you all have been around since the beginning of the dark covens. I need to know if there is a way to neutralize or strip the covens of their powers."

Sarah looks more confused than ever. "*You're* a coven witch."

"I'm not like other dark witches, never have been. Neither was my mother." I tell her about my mother's attempt to flee the coven, her murder, and my determination to escape.

Sarah watches me, probably wondering if she can trust a word that comes out of my mouth.

"Eventually, the covens will find us, and they'll come after us. I don't think you want them returning to Salem any more than I do."

"We don't have the power to defeat the covens," Sarah says. "If we did, we would have done it long ago."

"I think maybe I do."

"One witch?"

"How about one white witch?"

Sarah's eyes widen as I tell her about what happened at Shiprock. "Not everything I took from the earth that night was good though. There's a new darkness inside me, separate from what's always been there."

"Tell me about it."

So I do. "Can you help me?"

Sarah hesitates for a moment, possibly still letting everything I've thrown at her sink in. "Perhaps."

I start to take a step. "Great, let's get to it."

Sarah holds up her hand. "Not so fast."

"Time isn't likely something we have a lot of."

"We have spent our entire existence hiding from your kind. I'm not about to invite you in with open arms without checking out your story." She glances around and seems to make eye contact with someone. Amanda? Another member of the Bane? How many of them have been watching us this entire time?

"If what you say is true, we have a lot to discuss," she continues. "I'll be in touch."

"When?" I ask as Sarah starts to walk away.

"You'll know when you hear from me."

I growl under my breath, fighting the urge to follow her and demand answers now.

Keller takes my hand. "We're a lot closer than we were a few minutes ago."

"Not close enough."

Chapter Nine

Just because we have to wait for Sarah to make the next move with the Bane doesn't mean there aren't things we can do to prepare for an eventual showdown with the covens. We all decide to dedicate mornings to research and afternoons to training. With Rule's help, we find an abandoned piece of property far from the nearest neighbors.

"Old man Gantry died about five years ago," Rule says as he rounds the front of his car next to a weathered, two-story house. "His kids live in New York. I don't think anyone ever comes here anymore. Not sure why they don't sell it, but it's a good thing they haven't."

Keller pops open the cover on the bed of his truck, eliciting a whistle from Egan. "I'm impressed," Egan says as he slaps Keller on the back. Even though he's still not talking to Toni, Egan seems to have made up with Keller.

One step at a time, I guess.

When I reach the back of the truck, I see the source of Egan's appreciation. A wide assortment of guns, knives, bags of rock salt, swords and rope fill the truck. "Wow, Hunters R Us seems to be in business," I say.

Toni reaches into the truck bed and retrieves a pistol.

Before he thinks, Egan reaches for her hand. "Careful. You'll kill yourself with that thing."

"Guess you wouldn't have to worry about the covens doing it then, would you?"

Whoa. I don't recognize this Toni, and from the stunned look on his face Egan doesn't either.

"That's not fair," he says.

Toni shrugs. "Life's not fair." She steps back from Egan and walks away. She doesn't stalk as if she's angry, and she doesn't look sad. More like she's erased any feelings at all where Egan is concerned.

Egan looks dumbfounded as he watches Toni's retreat. I know he wants nothing more than to go after her and take her in his arms, but he doesn't let himself.

I meet Keller's eyes, and he shakes his head slowly. We've got to let Toni and Egan figure this out, but it's hard to stand by and do nothing.

While the guys unload the truck, Toni and I start constructing targets by placing soda cans atop the fence posts that line the edge of the property behind the house.

"Toni?" I say as we work side by side.

"Yeah?"

"Are you okay?"

"Will be when I get the hang of all these weapons."

"That's not what I mean."

"Oh, you mean Egan." She shrugs. "Yeah, fine. What's done is done."

"Are you sure it's done?"

She looks at me then, and beyond the resolve I see a tinge of sadness in her eyes. "Couldn't be more done."

I don't believe it. I don't believe she believes it. And despite his mulish determination to keep himself apart, I know Egan doesn't believe it. I just have no idea how to fix things. At the moment, I feel more capable of taking on my coven again than mending the rift between my friends. I hate feeling helpless.

You're not helpless. I gasp at the loudness of that voice in my head.

"What's wrong?" Toni asks.

I lift my hand to my head. "It's nothing."

"Don't lie to me."

I take a slow, deep breath, but the darkness doesn't want to retreat. I feel as if it's giving me an evil smile.

Stop resisting.

"Sometimes I just feel like I'm losing my grip. This darkness inside me . . . I'm scared it's going to win. It feels like it has a mind of its own."

Toni takes my hands in hers. "It won't rule you. You won't let it. I won't let it. You've come too far."

I force a smile. "You're a good friend, better than I deserve."

"I could say the same thing, but then it would just turn into the world's silliest conversation. Let's just say we're both really lucky."

I nod. "Deal."

When the guys drop the final bags of weapons on the ground, it's time for the lessons to begin. I watch as Keller demonstrates how to fire the various guns. It makes him look powerful, in control, perfectly capable of keeping himself safe. And sexy. It makes him look very, very sexy.

"Careful, your drool is showing," Toni says next to me.

She doesn't fare much better though when Egan takes a turn, though she tries really hard to hide her yearning. I open my mouth to say something but then remember there's evidently nothing I can say to make things better. Only time will tell whether Egan and Toni can find their way back to each other. I look at Keller and am profoundly glad that we're not at odds anymore.

"Despite the fact I won't need to use a gun, I have to admit that's sort of a rush," Egan says.

"They're not toys," Keller says, probably echoing something his father told him years ago.

"Neither are these." Egan holds up his hands and lets a little bit of power arc between his fingertips.

"That doesn't get any less freaky each time I see it," Rule says.

"And we don't need to be seeing it," I say, reminding Egan that we're here to train in conventional weaponry since we can't exactly practice with our full powers.

"Your turn," Keller says as he looks at me.

It's odd how I have a huge well of deadly power within me, but the thought of the bullets inside the pistol give me the wiggins. Yes, I shot that spirit back in Baker Gap when I was out with Keller, but that was different. The gun had been loaded with rock salt for getting rid of spirits, not projectiles that could kill humans. Am I ready for that? Killing people?

The darkness seems to double in size within me, pushing at its confines, demanding to be set free. To kill. My breath catches halfway up my throat at how suddenly the darkness has bloomed to full life, like it's tired of waiting around for me to give in. I shake my head, wondering if it's just some mixed-up side effect of my white witch power mixing with the dark, a need to protect twisting into its opposite. I've got to figure out how to separate the two and banish the darkness.

I need for Sarah to give me answers and fast, before it's too late.

"You okay?" Keller asks as he takes my hand.

The darkness lessens, but it doesn't go away. It's like a dog fighting against a leash, doing its best to break free. That scares me. Really, really scares me.

"Jax?"

I look up at Keller and see his concern. If he's going to be a part of any fight that's coming, he doesn't need to be worrying about me. He needs to keep all of his focus on staying safe. "Yeah. Kind of silly to be freaked out by a gun, isn't it?"

"No, not really. It's not part of who you are."

Not like the dark half of my power.

"Here, I'll help you." Keller places the pistol in my hands, shows me how to hold it, then steps behind me to help me aim. "Just take your time. Best to learn how to do it right slowly so that you can do it quickly when you need to without even thinking."

We both know that when the time comes, I won't be using a pistol or any of the other weapons he's brought along. I'm a weapon, a lethal one. The surge of joy at that knowledge causes my heart to skip a beat. Is that joy a result of acknowledging I'm powerful and may be able to defeat the covens or of the idea that I can be lethal? I fear it's the latter. The darkness is getting more restless, more relentless in its effort to make me cave.

Leave me alone! I don't say it out loud, but the scream in my head sounds like cannon fire. It bounces around and reverberates throughout my entire body. Before I realize what is happening, a surge of power has traveled down my arm and causes the gun to fire amid a shower of sparks. The can on the post is obliterated, and I'm pretty sure it's not the bullet that caused its demise. Smoke rises from the top of the charred post.

"I'm sorry," I say. I drop the gun and walk away.

"Jax." Keller tries to follow me, but I hear Egan telling him to let me go. Keller shoves Egan aside and catches up to me, but he doesn't grill me with questions. He's just there, a supportive presence.

I don't know how long I walk, but by the time I stop and look back we're on top of a hill looking down on the farmstead. Our friends continue to practice what Keller has already shown them.

"What is it?" Keller asks.

I take a long, deep breath. "I'm struggling more and more with what feels like evil inside me. It feels like I've got a split personality, and my evil side is getting closer to taking over."

"We won't let that happen. You're strong, Jax, stronger than anyone I've ever met. And we'll get help from the Bane, whatever they can offer."

"If it doesn't come too late. What if Sarah decides it's more important to keep the Bane hidden and they disappear completely?"

"Then we'll deal with that just like we have everything else."

I shake my head slowly and blink against tears. "I don't want to hurt anyone. Or worse."

Keller steps forward and takes my hands, urging me to look up into his eyes. "Don't worry about what-ifs. Focus on right now, fighting this moment only. That's how we get through."

I want to believe him that I'll be strong enough to keep fighting the good fight, but I have to make plans for if I fail. I slip my hands out of his and take a few steps away from him. "I need you to promise me something."

"What?" Keller asks, wary.

"I need to know that if I lose the battle you'll do what's necessary."

Keller shifts from one foot to the other. "What do you mean?"

"You don't have to ask that. You know. You've been doing it since you were a boy."

Anger floods his face. "I'm not going to kill you."

"Even if I threaten your life?"

"You're stronger than it, Jax. You won't hurt me."

"You willing to bet Toni's life on that?"

He props his hands on his hips. "Why are you asking me this?"

"Because I don't trust anyone else to do it. I can't stand the idea of becoming like the rest of my coven. I'd rather be dead."

"Don't say that."

"Why not? It's true."

Pain replaces the anger, tugging at the angles of the face I love. Keller steps toward me and wraps his hands around my upper arms. "What you're asking, I can't do it. We'll find a way to defeat this."

I pull away. "That's what I want, more than anything. But I have to be smart about this. If I succumb to this darkness . . ." I motion toward my middle and grimace. "I don't want to kill people, Keller. Not the people I love, not innocents I don't even know."

"You don't have it in you to kill."

"You want to believe that, but you know that capacity is in me. There's something else that isn't me but it's living inside me like a parasite. It wants to take over, destroy whatever white magic I might have briefly accessed."

Keller rubs his hand over his face and stalks several steps away. Without looking at me, he asks, "How am I supposed to promise this? I can't even imagine it."

"Because it's who you were born to be, a protector. You're good at it, and if it comes to it you have to take me out just like you would any other supernatural threat."

He looks at me, and I see tears shining in his eyes. He shakes his head.

"You'll do it because the fate of the world is more

important than my one life," I say. "I won't be able to live with myself if I give in to this darkness, so you'll do this for me because you love me."

He turns away, and I think it's because he's lost the war with his tears. I let him hide them from me. It's enough to know that he cares enough to shed them.

Time seems to slow to a glacial pace as I watch the rise and fall of his breathing. Finally, he nods. He can't say the words, but he's agreed. When he turns around, I think he's headed back down the hill. Instead, he closes the space between us and pulls me into his arms.

"I will fight this, Jax. I'll fight it with everything in me," he says.

"I will, too."

His lips come down on mine, insistent and scared and full of need. I wrap my arms around his neck and kiss him back with all the love I feel for him, with the hope I have that I will defeat the darkness.

The next morning, Keller looks like he's aged ten years as we head out for another long day. I suspect I look no better. Actually, we're all looking a little more than rough around the edges. If the covens don't finish us off, stress and fatigue might. Because Rule is out of school for the Thanksgiving break, we decide to do our training first.

As usual, Toni rides with Keller and me, and Egan drives his own vehicle. There's still been no thaw between Egan and Toni, and I'm beginning to lose hope.

When Rule arrives, I can tell something is different as he approaches.

"What's wrong?" I ask.

"Sarah came to see us this morning asking lots of questions about you and Egan."

My anger flashes, and the dark entity inside me snaps like a rabid dog. "Is she still there?"

"No. She left the same time I did."

"What did she want to know?" Egan asks.

"If we thought you were trustworthy, if you'd shown any evil tendencies, how you knew about the Bane."

"What did you all say?"

"The truth. Grandma was honest about everything, but she told Sarah that she expected her to help you in return. And that if Sarah and the Bane did anything to try to hurt you, she'd do whatever she could to make sure they were sorry."

"Fiona threatened a witch?" Egan said.

Rule turns his attention to him. "More than one. We found out that there are more than Sarah and Amanda, but not too many. Sarah wouldn't be specific. I got the feeling she's still finding it difficult to believe that not one but two coven witches could defect."

"Did she reveal anything else?"

Rule's gaze shifts back to me. "She said that if you are truly a white witch, you are the only one. And that they are discussing how to progress. Evidently, there is some history to white witches, but not in the lifetime of any of the current Bane. She did have one message for you."

"That she couldn't deliver herself?" I snap.

Rule shrugs. "She said it was extremely important that you resist the new darkness you took in at Shiprock."

"Like I'm not trying."

"She told us that white witches are rare, and they don't want to run the risk of losing you to the dark forces."

"Then why don't they just stop hiding and help me?"

"They plan to, but Sarah said they had to make some preparations first."

I make a sound of disgust, causing Keller to grip my shoulder.

"There's nothing we can do on that front right now," he says. "So let's just do what we came out here to do and go from there."

After a frustrated moment, I nod. Maybe I can work off some of the edgy energy vibrating within me. This morning, we practice with knives and swords. Toni is surprisingly good at throwing knives, so much so that even Egan looks impressed.

"You might want to be nicer to her," Rule says. "She could just decide you look like a good target to practice on." He's become more and more a part of our group every day. Sometimes I still catch him staring at me, but for the most part we've gotten past that awkward attraction.

Egan ignores him, but there's a suspicious glint in Toni's eyes. I hope she's not thinking too hard about what Rule just said.

When Rule catches my gaze, he shrugs. I realize he's trying to help Egan and Toni because he knows Keller and I can't. I smile at him then refocus my attention on the sharp knife in my hand.

Use it.

I shake my head against the insistent voice inside me. I wonder if this is what going crazy feels like.

"It's bothering you again?" Toni asks.

"There's no *again* about it. It's there more often than not now." I glance at Keller, remembering what I made him promise me.

"Let's go back to town," she says. "I've had enough of this for today."

I agree. I'd rather talk to Fiona and Adele about their conversation with Sarah, maybe track Sarah down and tell her I'm tired of waiting for answers.

The guys aren't happy with cutting the training session short, particularly Rule, but they come along nonetheless.

When we reach the herb shop, we descend the stairs to the basement as usual. But today the smells are different. Instead of the overriding scents of earth and old books, the aromas of roasted meat, freshly baked bread, and pumpkin greet us. When we reach the bottom of the stairs, the books and papers have been cleared away from the table to be replaced with a Thanksgiving feast. A golden turkey is surrounded by bowls of mashed potatoes, green beans, cornbread dressing, fresh cranberry sauce and bright green peas. Pumpkin, chess and pecan pies round out the offerings.

I glance at Rule and remember he was the one to suggest we train first today. "You knew about this, didn't you?"

"Hard to miss all the banging around in the kitchen this morning."

"You look stunned," Fiona says as she walks toward us, looking from me to Egan and back. "Both of you."

"We . . ." I choke on my words. "We've never had a Thanksgiving before."

"The covens aren't in the habit of thanking anyone for anything," Egan says. I can tell he's touched by the gesture, too.

Fiona reaches out and clasps one of my hands and one of Egan's. "Well, consider this the beginning of a new tradition for you then."

It's so tempting, but I remember why I came here. "I need to talk to you about Sarah Davenport's visit this morning."

"There's nothing to say beyond what I'm sure Rule already told you. Your arrival in Salem surprised the Bane just as much as it did us. You have to understand the suspicion. Their ancestors were hurt by the covens, sent into exile. They want to make sure this isn't a trick to draw them out."

"You trusted us."

"Yes, we did. After some tests and getting to know you a little," Fiona says. "And now it's time for you to trust me. I believe Sarah is a good woman and is only trying to look out for what remains of the Bane. She did tell me that she truly hopes you are a white witch because that would change everything."

"But how? I want specifics."

"You'll find out soon." Fiona squeezes my upper arms. "But not now. Now we eat and give thanks for all the positive things in our lives. For a couple of hours, let's set aside all the fear and doubt and anger and enjoy each other's company."

I glance at the table laden with food, and I'm touched all over again. I step forward and take Fiona in my arms, hugging her like I'd once hugged my mother. "Thank you. You have no idea how much this means."

Fiona leans back and frames my face with her weathered hands. "I think maybe I do. Now, come on. Let's eat. I've been smelling this all morning, and I'm starving."

I smile and join my friends at the table. Egan looks a bit hesitant, but he finally sits down across from me. He has an expression of disbelief on his face. I understand where it's coming from. When we defected from the covens, we knew that it might mean a life alone or perhaps just the two of us. Finding Keller and Toni was a miracle. To expand our circle of friends to even more people we care about seems like more of a bounty than all the food before us. I know from the stirring of his emotions that he feels the same way I do—that he'd give his life for the people surrounding us, any one of them.

From the first bite, I'm in heaven. The guys put away an impressive amount of food, but I have to admit I'm not far behind them. "This is delicious," I say after finishing my last bite of pumpkin pie.

"This is the best meal I've ever had," Egan adds.

"I'm sure you've both had better meals," Fiona says. "Money buys some mighty fancy food."

"Fancy doesn't equal good," I say. Sure, our coven's chef, Hiram, was a master in the kitchen. But I doubt he ever put one bit of love into anything he cooked.

Egan leans back from the table and pats his flat stomach. "Now I think I could sleep for a week."

"Unfortunately, we don't have that luxury," Toni says as she starts stacking plates.

"Honey, I can do that," Fiona says.

"No, we'll help," I say, wanting to preserve the good mood even if that means getting Toni out of the room for a bit.

Rule takes what is left of the turkey up the stairs, followed by his mother and grandmother with leftovers in each hand.

After Toni disappears with a load of dirty dishes, I turn to Egan and speak quietly. "If you can't manage it any other day, at least be nice to Toni today."

Egan throws up his hands. "What did I do?"

"Ignored her just like you do every other day."

"We've had this conversation."

My temper snaps as I jab my index finger at him. "You need

to stop being so selfish and just tell her the truth. In case you haven't noticed, she's spending her holiday away from her family for you."

I expect him to argue, but he seems to deflate instead. I don't wait to see if he says anything else, instead grabbing the rest of the dirty dishes and heading for the stairs. "Wipe the table down, and get ready to work," I say over my shoulder. "We're going to power through the rest of this material and find every scrap we can on white witches and the Bane. I want to know what the connection between the two is."

I hear a grumble from Egan, but I can't make out the words. They really don't matter.

When I reach the top floor, I meet Rule as he heads back downstairs. Fiona is already loading the dishwasher while Adele and Toni rearrange the contents of the refrigerator to accommodate the leftovers.

"Ah, good, give me those," Fiona says. She takes the dishes from my hands and fills up the final slots in the dishwasher.

"Thank you again," I say. "Everything was wonderful."

"If you'd like, I can teach you how to cook."

I open my mouth to ask if Egan told her about my severe lack of cooking prowess, but I don't want to upset Toni any more by even saying his name. "When all this is over, I might just take you up on that."

It touches me deeply that she would offer something so personal, something that is passed down to daughters and granddaughters. I'm someone she barely knows. My heart squeezes at how I'd so often imagined doing things like cooking with my mom, but that possibility was ripped away with a brutality that set me on the path I'm currently trudging down. I look at Fiona's profile and experience a swell of affection for her. It's all I can do not to pull her into my arms and hug her silly.

When we finish cleaning the kitchen, I notice Toni staring out the window. "You okay?"

She lets out a long breath. "Actually, I don't feel like doing research today. I know we need all hands on deck, but . . ."

I wrap my arm around her shoulders. "You don't have to work every waking hour."

"You do."

"It's my fight. I'm the one who started all this by running away."

Toni leans her head on my shoulder. "I want to help, really I do. I just can't go back down there and pretend that nothing's wrong. It's ripping me apart inside."

I squeeze her harder and lean my cheek against her head. "I know. I haven't given up hope that he'll come around."

"I can't afford to hope that anymore," she says. "It hurts too much." She pulls away and stares out the window again. It's a beautiful day if cold, but it does nothing to lift Toni's mood. "I just need some time alone."

I squeeze her hand. "Okay. I'll be just downstairs if you need anything."

That coaxes a small smile from her. "Since it's Thanksgiving, I want you to know that I'm thankful for you. You're the best friend I've ever had."

I pull Toni back into my arms for a long hug. "I feel the same way about you."

"If you want to lie down or watch TV, feel free," Adele says.

I realize that Adele's frosty exterior has melted some in recent days. Maybe she's finally seen how serious we are about making a positive change.

"Thanks," Toni says. "I think I'll sit outside for a bit, get some fresh air." She heads for the door and goes downstairs to the main level.

I stare after her for several seconds.

"It's a hard thing, watching people we love hurt so much," Fiona says.

"Yeah. The frustrating thing is that Egan loves her, and he's never actually loved a girl before."

"But he wants to protect her." Fiona doesn't ask it. She knows.

I nod. "I think he's doing more harm than good."

"They'll figure things out."

I look at Fiona. "What makes you think so?"

"I'm pretty observant," she says with a hint of a smile. "And those two watch each other when they don't think the other will notice."

"Mom is a firm believer in things turning out the way they should," Adele says with equal parts affection and doubt.

"It's true."

Adele laughs a little. "Yes, but it was annoying when I fell and broke my arm skateboarding, and you said, 'Everything happens for a reason.'"

"And as I recall, you met your prom date in the ER that day."

"Details, details." Adele gives her mom a one-armed hug then heads back downstairs.

I start to follow her but notice a framed cross-stitch pattern on the wall. It has a deep green background with a Celtic knot stitched in gold thread. "This is pretty."

"It is, isn't it? Adele made that for me for Mother's Day one year." Fiona steps up beside me and traces her finger through the air over the five interconnecting circles. "The four outer circles represent the elements. Earth, fire, water, air. The one in the middle connects them all. Together, it represents balance."

I think back to Sarah's bracelet, my earrings and belt buckle, wondering if they're Celtic in origin. "If I drew a symbol, do you think you might be able to tell me what it means?"

"Possibly." She indicates a pad of paper and pen on the countertop.

I fold back a grocery list in progress and draw the double spiral. When I'm finished, I turn the notepad so it faces Fiona.

"That's also a symbol of balance. Where did you see it?"

"My mother gave me a belt buckle and earrings with that symbol. And then the other day I saw it on a bracelet Sarah Davenport was wearing."

"Could be just a coincidence. Celtic symbols are popular even among people who have no Celtic ancestry."

I look down at the symbol. "I'm not a big believer in coincidences."

"Perhaps it's not. We did come across that passage about a balance in nature. Then there are the dark and light sides to you, to all of us really. Maybe you're the one who will find that perfect balance within yourself or be the one to bring balance."

Suddenly, the idea of having that much responsibility makes me exhausted. But there is still plenty of work to be done. If there's an answer in the basement about how the Bane and white witches are connected, I intend to find it.

Fiona pats my cheek. "You'll figure it out, sweetie."

I follow her back downstairs. When I reach the basement, Egan meets my eyes then looks behind me.

"Where's Toni?" he asks.

"She went outside for a bit."

"Alone?" There was no disguising the concern.

"Yes, and I think she wants to keep it that way for a while. She's right outside."

Egan is on the verge of bolting when Fiona steps behind him and places her hands on his shoulders. "Give her some time. You'll know the right moment to tell her how you feel."

Egan opens his mouth, but no protest comes out. Has he finally decided to give in and stop holding Toni at arm's length? My hope that this is the case increases an hour later when Egan asks if anyone wants anything to drink and heads for the stairs. This after he's looked at the stairs at least two dozen times in the past hour.

Everyone passes on his offer, and I smile as I watch him bound up the stairs.

I glance back at all the material we still have to sift through, frustrated that I've found no more references to the Bane or white witches. When I realize we've covered way more than we have left, that's exciting but also worrisome. Why can't a big, blinking, neon sign show up in the sky pointing me toward what I need? Answers about the Bane and what exactly being a white witch means. Toward the missing page of the Beginning Book and whatever mystery it holds. If I go through the rest of this and find nothing, I fully intend to hunt down Sarah Davenport and tell her she has no choice but to tell me everything.

"Do you think he's finally tired of being a jackass?" Keller asks as he looks toward the door at the top of the stairs.

"Guess we're about to find out." I refocus on the text in front of me.

We all jump when the door at the top of the stairs bangs open. Power springs to life at my fingertips as I push back my chair and stand in one motion. It's Egan, but he looks panicked.

"She's gone," he says.

"What?" Keller says, instantly alert.

But Egan has already left the empty doorway in his wake. I race up the stairs with Keller on my heels and everyone else following. I find Egan outside, scanning the area surrounding the shop.

Egan points at me, and his eyes go dark. "You left Toni alone, and now she's gone."

My heart drops a moment before my own power leaps to attention, turning me into a living, breathing electrical storm. I've got to find Toni. And then I'll kill whoever took her.

Chapter Ten

"Jax, Egan, calm down," Keller says as he reaches a hand out to both of us.

The voice inside my head is yelling so loudly that I can barely hear him. And I definitely don't want to heed his urging to calm down.

She's gone, and it's your fault.

Keller takes a step toward me, and I spin toward him with my hand outstretched to blast him. I stop myself just in time. He's not successful in hiding his fear before I see it. What am I doing? With great effort, I quell my power enough to stop the charges arcing at my fingertips. I can't, however, purge myself of the guilt. Why hadn't I come out here with Toni? Told her she needed to stay inside?

"What's going on, guys?"

I spin and look behind me on the sidewalk. Toni stands there with a takeout coffee cup in one hand and a bag from the pharmacy in the other.

Egan stalks past me but pulls himself up short before he gets to her. He takes a moment to shut down his power surge, but his anger doesn't lessen one bit. "Where the hell have you been?"

She gives him an annoyed eye roll. "To get coffee and some hair color, not that it's any of your business," she says.

"It is my business!"

"I fail to see why." She takes a sip of her coffee, which only seems to fuel Egan's anger.

"We thought you'd been taken," he says.

"I was a block up the street. It's not like I'm stupid enough to go off somewhere by myself."

Fiona pats Toni's shoulder. "We're glad you're okay,

honey." Then she and Adele go back inside.

Toni glances at Egan. "You look like you've got an uncomfortable bunch in your drawers."

Egan makes a growling sound of frustration. "You make me crazy."

"I could have sworn you didn't think about me at all."

"Oh, my God, woman, you are so dense. I think about you all the time."

Toni stops lifting her coffee cup to her mouth for another drink, a mixture of hope and doubt reflected in her eyes. "You do? Why?"

I feel the barriers fall inside Egan. "Because I love you, damn it." He stalks forward and pulls Toni into his arms. She drops the paper cup on the path and wraps her arms around his neck.

The dark aspects of Egan's power recede, proof that Toni's touch has the same effect on him that Keller's does on me. That's something else I need to ask Sarah about if she ever deigns to show her face to me again.

They kiss for so long and with so much passion that I grow embarrassed. When I glance at Keller, he smiles then laughs under his breath. "I'm thinking I want to be elsewhere. How about you?"

"Lead the way."

We return to the basement and go back to work. Adele and Fiona stay on the main level, preparing stock for the busy Christmas shopping season. Tired of sitting, I grab the book I was scanning and read some more while pacing around the room. A few minutes go by before Rule says, "Finally."

I look up and see him smiling. "Tell me you found something useful."

"Only the names of Penelope's missing friends."

"Really?" I drop my book and rush forward to stand behind him. I look at his surprisingly pretty handwriting. Who has pretty handwriting anymore?

"In a book of New England legends of all things. It seems that beginning soon after the girls disappeared, the legends began that they were all dead and haunting the woods around Salem. Over time, it turned into a story meant to scare kids on camping trips. 'Be good or the dead witches will get you.'"

I stare at the names—Jane Burkes, Elizabeth Woodley, and Vera Dewey. I reach past Rule's shoulder and point toward Vera's name. "I think I saw a Dewey in the cemetery where Penelope's crypt is."

"Let's go see if it's her, and if the others are there. Determine if their graves are spelled, too."

"I could stand doing something else for a while," Keller says.

Rule stands. "Let me get my coat. Oh, and don't mention where we're going to my grandmother or mom. They've been getting weirdly protective the past couple of days."

I share a glance with Keller. Are they getting the feeling that time is running out, too? That before long we are going to be facing off with more witches than we can count whether we have an effective defense or not?

I nod and we all head upstairs.

"Where are you all off to?" Fiona asks, sounding a bit too curious for our liking.

"Over to the cottage," Rule says as he grabs his coat from a hook on the wall.

"Okay, don't stay out too late."

"I won't," Rule says.

"And be careful."

I meet Fiona's gaze and I detect her meaning, that I'm supposed to protect her only grandchild from any harm. I give her a slight nod then follow Keller and Rule out of the shop.

Keller drives a tick below the speed limit so we don't draw attention. When he reaches the lane that leads to the cemetery, he switches off his headlights.

I find I'm holding my breath until we see that no other vehicles are here. Why I thought we'd roll up on Sarah out here in the dark, I can't say.

Keller retrieves three apocalypse-strength flashlights, the kind that can be used as a weapon as much as a way to light up the night. I guess when you're in the hunting evil business you can't risk your life on a crappy flashlight.

We approach the cemetery slowly, as if we're afraid the bogeyman is going to jump out and scare the life right out of us.

"You know, I might have a lot of power at my beck and call, but this place gives me the creeps," I say.

Rule pokes me in the side. I jump and scream like some twit in a horror movie. I swat him on the shoulder. "Not good to scare a coven witch."

Rule sobers. "Sorry."

We each take a row and examine the names that are still legible. I'm halfway down my row when I find what I'm looking for. "Here it is." I squat in front of the simple old stone. I reach out to touch the etched letters but hesitate with my fingers just an inch from the word "Dewey." What if this stone blasts me the way the crypt did? I survived that jolt, but it wasn't what you'd call pleasant.

Keller says my name just as I touch the stone. I sigh in relief when nothing happens. It feels like nothing more than the cold slab of stone that it is. I let my fingers drift over Vera's name. That's when I notice the small Celtic double spiral etched under her name.

"Look familiar?" I ask as I look up at Keller.

"Sarah's bracelet."

"And the belt buckle and earrings my mother gave me. This isn't a coincidence. It means something, a connection between us."

"I found Jane Burkes," Rule says from a couple rows back. "And Elizabeth Woodley is here, too."

My heart rate kicks up when I see the same Celtic symbol etched into their headstones. "Fiona said it's a symbol of balance."

"Seems to be a running theme," Rule says. "Was there one on the crypt?"

"I didn't see one, but maybe it's so small I missed it."

Rule heads toward the back of the cemetery. "Let's check it again."

"Be careful. My last inspection didn't end well," I say.

He turns toward me, though I can't make out his expression with only the faint glow of his flashlight. "We know you can't touch it," he says. "But what about us?"

"No, it's too dangerous." I hurry toward him. "If it burned my fingers, I don't like the idea of what it might do to you." I glance over at Keller, who has followed me. "Either of you."

"How likely do you think it is that the magic is going to work on normal humans?" Rule asks. "Don't you think someone would have touched it during all these years and noticed when it knocked them flat on their butt?"

"We should both try," Keller says.

I meet his gaze. "You're not helping."

He walks past me. "Maybe I am. If it doesn't affect either of us, we'll know it's spelled to keep away coven witches."

"We still won't know why," I say.

"One less question is one less question," Keller says.

I sigh in defeat. Short of using my power to physically stop them, I know it's no use. They're going to do exactly what they want to, no matter what I say.

As we approach the crypt, the hairs on my arms stand on end. Whoever spelled Penelope's final resting place had powerful magic, like nothing I've seen outside of the covens. My stomach twists in knots, and I can't tell if it's the darkness stirring or simply my nerves. I stop several feet away from the crypt.

"I'll go first," Keller says. "Pretty sure no one in my family has ever been a witch."

I grow more anxious and a touch nauseated as Keller walks toward the crypt. All three of us shine our flashlights toward the front where the ornate sun provides the only adornment other than the Davenport name. In the dark, it looks more like tendrils or maybe the snakes undulating off Medusa's head.

"Well, here goes nothing," Keller says and quickly places his palm next to the sun.

Nothing happens, and I'm so relieved that I laugh.

"Guess it's my turn," Rule says. "Let's see if it likes a smidge of witch."

"Smidge, I like it," Keller says. "I think I'll call you that from now on."

Rule gives him a dirty look, which just makes Keller laugh. The laughter fades, however, as Rule steps close to the crypt. He must be at least a little worried because he takes a deep breath before lifting his hand and stretching his fingers. He looks back at me. "If this knocks me silly, you have to come up with a good story, or my mom's going to kill me."

"I'm sure we can come up with something interesting." Keller sounds like he's on the verge of laughing at whatever scenario is floating through his head.

"Just when I was beginning to like you," Rule says with a shake of his head. With another deep breath, he places his hand on the stone. Nothing happens.

"Shucks," Keller says.

Rule punches him playfully in the shoulder.

"Guess that shows exactly who isn't supposed to be messing with this crypt," I say.

Rule shines his light around the front edges. "You think it's to keep dark witches from bothering Penelope's body since she defected from them?"

I shrug. "Makes sense. I can totally see a dark witch taking revenge even after someone's dead. But why just Penelope? Why are the other women's graves not spelled?"

"Good question," Rule says.

"What kind of magic is this?" Keller asks.

"All I know is it's powerful, like coven powerful. And it tells me the Bane members do have power because I think this type of magic has to be renewed every so often. I doubt a protection spell would last more than three hundred years without some recharging."

Keller shines his flashlight at the sun emblem on the front of the crypt then steps closer to it. "That symbol is on here, too, small and worked into the design of the sun so you have to be looking to see it."

I try to step closer to see it, but as soon as I do the darkness inside me goes on full alert and all of the hair on my arms stands on end. My long hair even starts to lift away from my scalp. Frustration pulses within me and next to it a powerful urge to do damage to the crypt, to demand entry. I'm still aware enough to know that last part isn't me. It's whatever has taken up residence inside me.

I clench my fists and teeth as I take a step back, trying to calm my reactions. Keller grips my hand, taking the edge off the darkest part of me.

"Here's what I don't understand," Rule says. "If Jax is a white witch, why is the spell repelling her?"

"Because she hasn't accessed her full powers."

We all spin toward the new voice. Power is already sizzling at my fingertips when I recognize Sarah Davenport stepping into the faint light shed by our flashlights.

Sarah stops a few feet away and meets my eyes. "If you have the potential to become a white witch, it's buried beneath what you've always been, a dark witch brought up within the confines of a dark coven."

"How do I access the white witch powers?"

"Determination. Think of it as a war within you, the darkness as your foe. There will be battles every day, victories, but also losses. You'll take ground only to lose it. But eventually one side will have to win. They cannot live side by side forever."

I fight an enormous wave of exhaustion, physical and mental. I'm not at all certain I have what it takes to fight this fight day after day.

As if he knows what I'm feeling, Keller takes my hand again and gives it a reassuring squeeze. I appreciate the effort, but it does little to bolster my confidence.

"How does she make sure she wins?" Rule asks.

Sarah glances toward him before returning her gaze to me. "By making sure that every decision she makes is not influenced by the darkness. The more she follows the path of the light, the closer she'll be to winning the war for supremacy inside her."

"She's already on that path," Keller says. "She left her coven, has protected her friends."

"She's also attacked those same friends." Sarah again glances at Rule. "She's lied. She's used magic to take over the minds of others."

I'm stunned that her investigation into my past has revealed so much, including the fact I used my power of influence to get a tourist to play my mother back in North Carolina so I could enroll in school.

"But she's not truly hurt anyone," Keller insists.

"It's not just the big decisions that matter. All the little decisions, no matter how small, add up." Sarah stares straight at me. "They are as much a part of who you are and who you will eventually become as life-and-death decisions."

Sarah takes a couple of steps, but I notice she stops at about the same distance from the crypt that I've chosen. "I can't touch it either. None of the Bane can."

"What's inside?" I ask.

"I don't know. All we know is that the Bane have been charged with keeping the spell in place since it was built."

I glance at the crypt. "Aren't you tempted to let the spell fade away and get a peek inside?"

Sarah gives me a hard look, and I realize that my words are being influenced by the darkness inside me.

"It was spelled for a reason," Sarah says. "I trust that it's a good one, even if it is no more than protecting Penelope's remains."

My instincts tell me it's much more than protecting a body, but either Sarah truly doesn't know or is choosing to not tell me. Can I really blame her? If the Bane have stayed hidden all these years, what kind of sense does it make for them to reveal their biggest secrets to someone who might very well turn out to be an enemy?

"So what now?" I ask.

"I'm willing to help you as much as I can, but ultimately it's up to you."

Which is more than a little scary since I feel a little less like me every day.

I try to be quiet the next morning when I leave my bedroom because Toni is still sleeping. She had a late night of talking and canoodling with Egan on the couch. They were curled up asleep when we returned from the cemetery, but she made her way to my bedroom sometime in the wee hours.

I'm surprised to see Egan is already sitting at the kitchen table with his laptop open, a huge mug of coffee next to him, and a perplexed look on his face.

"Didn't expect to see you up so early," I say as I slip a cinnamon pastry in the toaster. When he doesn't respond, I glance back. "What's wrong?"

"Maybe nothing. Maybe everything."

"That's specific."

He looks up at me then. "Do you think there are any other coven witches like us?"

"Ones who aren't totally evil?"

"Yeah. Maybe even ones who want to ditch their covens but don't know how?"

"I don't know," I say. "I would have bet money I was the only one until you showed up on my doorstep."

"And I didn't think it possible until you did it."

"Why are you asking?"

He taps the screen of the laptop. "I got an encrypted message at one of my e-mail addresses, one my family shouldn't know about. Someone is claiming he wants to join up with us."

I round the end of the table and read over his shoulder. It's a short message but one that poses a whole new set of questions.

Egan looks up at me. "What do you think?"

"I don't know what to think," I say. "Could someone else in your coven have sent it?"

"Anything's possible, but I doubt it. My firewalls have firewalls, and none of my family members are anywhere near as good with computers as I am."

"Still doesn't mean it's not a trap. Did you respond?"

He shakes his head. "Not sure I should, just in case."

I stare at the short message and wish I would get a gut feeling about it. "Nice to think we could increase our numbers on this side though."

"Three versus a gazillion instead of two versus a gazillion. I feel safer already."

But this message has me asking a lot of what-if questions. "Is there a way we can respond and keep ourselves safe? Like if you respond, will they be able to tell where you're at?"

"There are ways around that if you know how to do it."

"Do you?"

"I might be able to work some computer magic."

"I think it's worth finding out if this person is legit. And while you're at it, figure out a way to find out if there are others."

"That's a tall order," he says.

I squeeze his shoulder. "I have complete faith in your hacker genius."

He snorts but gets to work.

I pour a cup of coffee, retrieve my pastry and slip into the chair opposite him. "So, we went out to the cemetery again last night, and Sarah showed up."

"She sure likes that place."

"Seems it's full of former Bane members. She's also offered to help me try to access all my white witch powers if they're even still hanging around."

"How do you do that?"

"Seems it comes down to good decision-making for however long it takes to purge the darkness."

"Any idea how long?"

"Nope. Would be much easier to have some sort of cleansing ritual or something, but I guess that's too easy."

"Well, I guess you could start with the good decision to refill my coffee cup."

Instead, I toss a corner of my pastry at his head.

He dodges it and laughs. "Pretty sure that's a bad decision."

I know he's teasing, trying to ease my anxiety, but I have to wonder if maybe he's right. Does every move I make have to be pure as the driven snow? How exhausting. By the time I drive the darkness out, I may be too spent to fight the covens.

After finishing my breakfast, I head for the shower. But

when I enter the bedroom, Toni is awake, sitting in the middle of bed in a rumpled T-shirt from her *Firefly* collection. It sports the word "Shiny" in a metallic script. I motion toward the newly dyed streaks in her hair, purple where they used to be pink. "I like the purple, though it's going to take some getting used to."

"Yeah, felt like a change."

"Surprised you had time to do a dye job last night."

"Doesn't really take that long. Did it while Egan was ordering pizza and doing some work on the computer." She smiles. "Turns out you're not the only witch who likes the purple."

I stick my fingers in my ears and start saying, "La-la-la-la." I still hear Toni laughing at me. When I lower my arms, I grow more serious. "I'm glad for you both. It was about to kill me seeing you like that."

"I'm glad, too. But don't think that means I'm not going to make him pay for a while."

This time I laugh.

"What did you and Keller do last night?" Toni asks.

"Well, let's see. Rule found the names of the other missing witches, and the three of us went out to the cemetery where Penelope's crypt is. The original Bane members are there, too." I tell her about the Celtic symbols on all their grave markers and how Keller and Rule were both able to touch the crypt, thus proving that it's only spelled against dark witches. "And Sarah made an appearance to tell me I'm not a white witch, at least not yet."

Toni stares at me for a moment. "So, a boring evening then?"

"Even more boring this morning. Egan got a message from someone claiming to be another coven witch wanting to defect."

Her eyes widen. "You believe them?"

I shrug. "I don't know, but your boyfriend's doing some techy magic to see if it's legit or a trap."

Toni rubs her bare arms, and I'm pretty sure it has nothing to do with the weather outside. "How much danger do you really think we're in?"

The darkness twists in my middle. "More than I care to think about. If I can't access the full powers of a white witch before the covens find us, I wouldn't lay odds on us coming out of another fight alive."

Sudden banging on the bedroom door makes us both jump. "Guys, we need to talk," Keller says.

Toni and I look at each other before rushing for the door. When I open it, Keller is pacing across the room with a worried expression. Looks like it's going to be an eventful morning.

"That can't be good," Toni says.

"It's not," Keller says as he stops and stares at us. He holds up his phone. "Just got a text from Dad."

"And how is Señor Evil Hunter this morning?" Egan asks, his dislike of Rev. Dawes abundantly clear.

Keller spares Egan a quick look of annoyance. "Worried. The covens aren't our only problem anymore."

"I'm almost afraid to ask," I say.

"Seems Amos Barrow has taken an interest in you and Egan, and if Dad's source is right, Toni and me, too."

Toni utters a curse word I've never heard her say. I can't blame her. Though the covens have stayed off hunters' radar screens through strategic use of their powers—meaning killing any hunters who even got close to finding us, there isn't a witch alive who hasn't heard of Amos Barrow. He's only the most notorious hunter working today. Even the meanest poltergeists and vengeful spirits eventually fall to him.

Word is he doesn't have a soul, that he will kill anything not one hundred percent mortal human with not an ounce of remorse or the blink of an eye. Stories vary, but his kill tally is freakishly high. Some in the covens are even convinced he's a myth. Maybe he is because if he isn't, why haven't the covens taken him out of play long ago? But I'm not willing to stake my life or any of my friends' lives on him not being real.

For several stunned moments, we all just stare at each other.

"Did your dad say whether Barrow knows where we are?" I ask.

"He doesn't know."

The darkness churns within me at the thought of facing Barrow. It wants this fight, one it's certain it can win. I might want nothing to do with that darkness, but I don't plan to lose to Barrow either. And I'm not going to let this latest blow cause my friends to lose faith. We have to stay positive, confident we'll come out on top of whatever challenges come our way.

"Well, this is a pain, but we're going to keep doing what we're doing," I say. "Training with every kind of weapon we can get our hands on, researching every nook, cranny and lead we find. And if I don't have my full power under control when we have to fight, then we'll do the best we can." I just hope it's enough to keep us all alive.

"We need to warn Rule and his family," I say. "They may not have magic like us, but Amos Barrow doesn't recognize shades of gray."

Keller nods, and I feel his approval. He knows that in this moment my good side is winning the internal battle.

"We need to abandon the cottage," Egan says. "Too many places for a person to hide nearby."

He's right. A lot of the cottage's charm lies in the thick vegetation around it, vines and hedges and shrubs. It was perfect when we wanted to stay hidden. But those things also make it dangerous when you want to see your enemy coming in time to prepare.

"We need high ground with an unobstructed view," I say.

"Like where we've been training," Toni says.

"Exactly." I motion to our surroundings. "Let's pack up, make this a quick move."

Nobody says anything about the fact we're going to be breaking into the old farmhouse and becoming squatters. In the bigger picture, those trespasses are nothing. If the owners knew what we're trying to protect them, everyone, from, they might just give the house to us.

As we load up our few belongings, I call Rule and tell him about the latest development with Barrow.

"You could stay here," he says. "We have room."

"No. It's too dangerous. We're going to stay out at the

farm."

"Are you heading there now?"

"Yes."

"I'll meet you there."

I know he's going to resist what I say next but I say it anyway. "I want you to stay at home. You and your family don't even need to be seen talking to us, not when Barrow might be watching. We don't need to draw his attention to you all."

"But he's not going to be able to tell we're anything other than normal humans."

"I wouldn't put it past him to judge you guilty by association and not stop to ask questions. Just trust me, it's better this way."

Rule tries to argue more, but I don't budge. This feels like a right decision, and I hope it is. Rule, Fiona and Adele have done enough for us. I can't ask anything more, not when it puts them in danger.

Next I call Sarah and spill everything all over again.

"Do you think it's really safe for you and Egan to stay with your friends?"

I hate that she's asking me this, reminding me that every single decision I make will have an impact on whether I become a true white witch. It brings up all my old fears about losing Keller and Toni, and I wonder if my acceptance of their help in this fight was a wrong decision motivated by not wanting to leave them again. But then I think about when my father kidnapped them and had them at his mercy.

I shake my head. "Barrow and the covens already know about them. I won't leave them unprotected. I did that once, and they almost lost their lives." I take a deep breath. "It's too late for running away. That ship has sailed."

After Sarah says she will come by the farm later, we lock the cottage door behind us and head for the vehicles. Once at the farm, it takes Egan a microsecond to unlock the door with a tiny fizz of power. Inside, it's even more obvious that no one has lived here in a long time. A layer of thick dust coats every visible surface.

"We can clean some later," I say. "Right now, we train."

Rule ignores my warnings completely and arrives with Adele and Fiona.

"I told you to stay away," I snap when Rule approaches.

He points to Keller and Toni. "If they have the right to make their own choices, so do we."

I throw up my hands and walk away.

Egan and I make an unspoken decision to train well into the afternoon because our friends need to be as prepared as they can be. While Egan and Keller help the others, Sarah arrives and we explore the layers of power within me.

"What does it feel like?" she asks as we sit facing each other on the front porch, her seeming comfortable in only a light jacket and me bundled up as if I'm trekking along the polar ice caps.

"Sort of like smoke, really dark smoke. Sometimes it's more like a coiled snake. It feels like it's going to strike at anything that threatens it."

"Imagine yourself walking down a path through the smoke. If the snake is there, ignore him."

I close my eyes and do as she says. I resist the urge to cough when I think I actually smell smoke. It thickens, trying to block me from walking forward.

"What do you see?"

"Just darkness." Suddenly that darkness presses against me, choking me. But then Sarah's hands are there, taking mine. It's not the same calming effect as when Keller touches me, but it serves as an anchor to the world outside.

We keep at it all day with only occasional short breaks. By the time I think I might see a glimmer of light beyond the smoke, I'm spent.

"That's enough for today," Sarah says and releases my hands. "You're exhausted."

"When I open my eyes, I discover that I'm not only bone tired but also soaked in sweat despite the cold air.

"I know it'll be difficult, but try to get some good rest tonight. You're no good to yourself or anyone if you're so fatigued you can't even think straight."

When Sarah leaves, I manage to drag myself inside where I find Adele cleaning.

"How bad are things going to get?" she asks me without preamble.

"I don't know, but the potential for very, very bad is definitely there."

She turns away with a look of distress written across her features in bold strokes. "I can't lose Rule. I lost his father to cancer when Rule was small, and it about killed me. I can't imagine losing my son."

I place my hand on her shoulder. "I will do everything within my power to make sure he stays safe, that all of you do."

She looks at me and holds my gaze, assessing. "I believe you."

Adele doesn't know how much her confidence means to me, but it also frightens me. What if I fail her? Fail them all? What if I'm not strong enough? I mentally shake myself. Enough of the doubt. I have to believe with every fiber of my being that we will prevail.

As the light begins to wane, Adele and I go outside to where the others are repacking all the gear. I notice that Keller has shifted some of the weapons to Egan's Jeep. It strikes me that it really does look like we're preparing for war.

Chapter Eleven

We all have a renewed determination during training the next morning, all of us understanding that each tick of the clock brings us closer to the inevitable battle for our lives.

The darkness inside me knows it's fighting for its very existence, too, because it struggles to force me into bad decisions. Snapping at my friends, giving in to my anger as Sarah tries to help me navigate toward that elusive light. When I feel myself get closer to the light, a surge of happiness goes through me. "Yes!"

"Good progress," Sarah says. "But you're a long way from where you need to be."

"I know that," I snap, annoyed that she's throwing water on my flicker of success. When I realize what I've done, I sigh. "I'm sorry."

"Just keep working at it."

When Sarah leaves to go to work so she doesn't draw undue attention or suspicion from anyone who might notice, Rule walks up to me.

"Grandma said we should go through the rest of the material in the basement today while we have the chance."

"I'm not sure that's the best use of our time now. We found the Bane."

"Maybe we don't find anything, but maybe we do." He gestures behind him where the others are putting away the weapons. "Besides, we're about as good with all that as we're going to get."

I'm still not sure, but sitting out here waiting for attack holds little appeal, too.

"Do you really think Sarah's telling you everything?" Rule asks when I continue to hesitate.

"No."

"Then keep looking on your own. If nothing else, it shows her you're not just going to sit back and accept what snippets she gives you."

I like that idea. It gives me a surge of confidence. I step close to Rule and kiss him on the cheek. "Thank you."

"For what?"

"Everything."

After a couple of hours of mostly useless research, I pull the Ending Book to me and go over it again. But nothing new reveals itself. I know with absolute certainty that the answer to everything is on that missing page of the Beginning Book. I know Sarah doesn't fully trust me, but can I trust her enough to reveal we have the Beginning and Ending books?

Unable to sit still any longer, I go upstairs for a soda. Fiona is standing behind the front counter of the shop.

"Get tired of reading?" she asks as she ties a bundle of some herb together with a green ribbon.

"Yeah. We're pretty much done anyway. We'll be able to finish in a couple more hours."

Fiona pats the tall stool next to her. "Then come keep me company in between customers."

I slide onto the stool and point at the pile of herbs in front of her. "What is that?"

"Patchouli." She meets my eyes. "For warding off evil."

"Do things like that really work?"

"I seem to remember some tea that worked as it was intended."

I smile. "Good point."

"None of it is to the extreme of your powers, but it's what our families have used for centuries. Herbs, intuition, these were the things witches were meant to use for the benefit of others. We just have a closer connection with the earth."

I pick up a sprig of the patchouli and spin it between my fingers. "If by some miracle we find a way to end the coven threat for good, will you teach me about herbs?"

Fiona smiles. "I would love to."

Without her asking, I begin to help wrap bundles. "What will you do with these?"

"I'll have some in every room, and I want each of us to have a bundle with us at all times. Every little bit of help is important at this point."

"It won't help against someone like Amos Barrow. He's not supernatural."

"There are other ways of dealing with humans, not the least of which is the pistol I keep under the front counter."

The image of Fiona packing heat is so funny that I laugh. When I glance down at the bundle of patchouli in my hands, I freeze. "Are you sure this stuff works?"

"Are you worried because it's not making your hands melt or something equally gruesome?"

"Yes."

"You're not evil," Fiona says with a conviction that startles me.

"Then why did the tea affect me like it did?"

"You took it internally. And it attacked the darkness inside you that you've been fighting, not who you are as a person."

"I wonder sometimes if all my thoughts of being a white witch are just wishful thinking, that what happened at Shiprock was a fluke."

"Sarah believes enough to work with you, give you the benefit of the doubt."

"She doesn't have this darkness inside her. No one does. So no one can know what it feels like. Just me. What is that about?"

"Maybe it's a test to see if you're worthy, one I have no doubt you'll pass. As for the Bane, I suspect they still have dark magic within them but have found some way to mute it."

When I think about it, I realize that sounds right for the source of the odd signatures I detected. Magic but magic dampened to the point that it doesn't register as such. If they've been able to control their magic, maybe there's hope for me.

Fiona grabs my hand and squeezes. "You listen to me," she says. "Is there something inside you fighting to take over? Yes. But you haven't let it. The simple fact that you're fighting it tells me that you, the person you really are through and through, is not evil. Neither is Egan. So many people in your position would have given up long ago."

I bite my lip and stare into Fiona's pale blue-green eyes. "It's so hard."

"I know, sweetie. And it will be a battle. If you're a white witch and that's something that scares the covens, you'll be dealing with more power than anyone you know has. There may be the temptation to use it in the wrong way, maybe even thinking you're doing the right thing at the time. You might begin to think you don't have to take advice from others who aren't as powerful. But I have faith that you will make the right decisions in the end."

"How can you say that? You barely know me."

Fiona releases my hand and gestures toward the basement. "I've seen how hard you work, how much you want to find a way to keep everyone safe. I suspect you're even willing to sacrifice yourself."

"I am." I'm surprised when Fiona doesn't try to convince me otherwise. Instead of being hurt by that, it makes me like her even more. She sees the big picture that protecting so many is more important than a single life.

"Don't get me wrong. I don't want anything bad to happen to you," she says as if she's been reading my thoughts. "But sometimes heroes don't have a choice."

"I'm no hero."

"You will be. I feel it in my bones."

I don't argue with her. The darkness stirs, not liking the idea of me being a hero one bit.

"We've waited for an opportunity like this to rid the world of the covens for a very long time," Fiona says, adding another finished bundle of herbs to the basket at her side.

"But I haven't even found the way to make everything right." I can't hide my frustration.

"I think the answer is within you, and in your willingness to let others help you."

We tie up a few more bundles in silence. Despite my

boatload of worries, the simplicity of the task and the quiet surrounding us are nice.

"Tell me about your mother," Fiona says suddenly.

The familiar stab of pain hits me in the chest, but I find I do want to talk about her. "She was so beautiful, so kind, which of course was her downfall. The covens see kindness as a sign of weakness. We were constantly reminded that kindness brought our ancestors nothing more than death sentences. But Mom wasn't obvious about it, not with anyone but me. She kept herself under the radar except for her painting. She was incredibly talented, and she made herself useful to the coven by commanding top dollar for her work."

"What changed?" There's a soft, kind touch to Fiona's question. She knows the next part is difficult for me to recount.

"She tried to escape with my sister and me, but we were caught and brought back to the coven." I swallow hard against the lump rising in my throat. "They put her in a Siphoning Circle, a circle of rocks spelled with the ability to rip out a witch's power."

"They tortured her." It's not a question.

I nod. "No witch has ever lived to tell what it's like to be siphoned, but I saw it with my own eyes. My sister and I were forced to watch as a warning. If we hadn't been children, we would have been siphoned right alongside our mother." I pause, hearing the echoes of my mother's screams. "I imagine it must be like your body is being ripped to shreds from the inside out. First, they drain the witch's power, which by itself is excruciating. But even when my mother's power was gone, it wasn't enough for my father and the other leaders. Then they began draining her life force, and it was agonizingly slow. Eventually, her body just shut down." I blink against hot, fat tears. "I remember the exact moment the life went out of her eyes, and then she was gone."

"And you determined that someday you would leave."

I nod and have to swipe at an escaping tear. "If Egan and I are captured, they'll do the same to us."

"You have something your mother didn't—friends who

will help you until their dying breaths."

"I don't want anyone to die, not for me."

"It wouldn't be just for you. We have a chance to free the world from the covens' evil. If that's not worth dying for, I don't know what is."

I sit in silence, letting her words sink in for several seconds. "At first all I wanted was to be left alone to live a normal life. But that's not enough anymore." I take a deep breath and pull myself up straight. "Now I want nothing more than to find a way to make sure my friends are safe, that no one is ever harmed by a dark witch again."

Fiona's attention is diverted by a couple of customers coming into the shop. She greets them and waits until they wander away from the front counter before looking up at me. "I'm so sorry about your mother," she says. "No one should ever have to see something like that, especially when you're a child. But it's made you who you are, a young woman with a powerful sense of right and wrong. You will end this, Jax. I feel it more deeply than I've ever felt anything. And I will do whatever I can to help you."

I hold Fiona's gaze then smile past the sadness of the memories. "My mother would have liked you."

"And I have no doubt I would have liked her, too. She would be proud of you."

I like that idea. I like it a lot.

I walk through the night dressed all in black, the thick folds of my dress flowing around me in the wind. My eyes are as dark as coal. I must be terrifying to behold, and that makes me smile. Another woman makes the mistake of stumbling into my path and I send a blast of power into her body, making her bow backwards for a moment before falling to the ground dead.

Suddenly, there are people everywhere, staring in disbelief at me, evil incarnate. I kill them indiscriminately. Men, women, even children. A familiar voice cries in the night and I stalk toward it, electricity arcing at my fingertips. When I see him, I feel nothing. Only when I send the full force of my power barreling into him, ripping his insides apart, do I smile. When he's almost dead, I let him drop to the ground and walk toward him. As I look down into Keller's agonized face, he only has enough strength to utter one word.

"Why?"

"Because I can." And then I finish his pitiful little existence.

I jerk awake with my heart hammering. I suck in deep breaths then cover my face with my shaking hands as I fight tears. I lie there, forcing my heart rate to slow, telling myself it was just a dream. A horrible, horrible dream. It's a miracle I don't wake Toni. Finally, unwilling to slip back into another terrifying nightmare, I slide out of bed and go into the living room. Keller is stretched out on the couch asleep, so I'm quiet as I make my way out to the front porch. Once I'm standing at the edge, I close my eyes as the memory of killing Keller in the dream comes back with too much clarity. The worst part is that I'd enjoyed it, relished it as I watched his life drain away.

When I force myself to open my eyes, I stare out across the farm as the first rays of sunlight break through the fog hanging low to the ground. Is Amos Barrow out there watching and planning his move?

The door opens but I don't turn to see who it is. It only takes a couple of steps for me to know it's Keller.

"You're up early," he says as he wraps his arms around me from behind.

"Couldn't sleep. Keep having nightmares." I don't tell him that my nights have been filled with nightmares for a while now. I dream about Mom's death, witches being burned at the stake, but nothing compares to the dream I'd just escaped. "I just want it all to be over."

He kisses my temple. "I know."

I take a deep breath and step away from him. The images in the dream don't fade. Neither does the feeling of immense power coursing through me. I pace, unable to stand still. I reach for the light magic within me to try to calm down, to remind myself that I'm not that evil person in the dream. But fear shoots through me when I can't find the light, no matter how hard I try.

"What's wrong?"

I tell him, and he pulls me into a firm hug. "You're tired and upset. Just give yourself a little time."

Concerned, I call Sarah, but she doesn't answer her cell or house phones. She's not at the library either, all of which only agitates me more. It doesn't help that as we spend the day with weapons training, I notice Keller watching me with concern in his eyes. That concern is not unwarranted, but it grates on my already raw nerves nonetheless.

In the afternoon, we go to town for a hot meal at the Soup Cauldron and to talk strategy. We map out how we might handle things if we face various scenarios—my coven, both Egan's and my covens, Barrow alone, multiple hunters. But no matter how much we talk, I can't shake the nightmare from this morning or the overwhelming feeling of foreboding.

Keller calls his dad, but Rev. Dawes hasn't heard anything else about Barrow.

"He asked Toni and me to come home. Aunt Carol is worrying herself sick over Toni," Keller says.

I set my spoon down carefully next to my bowl. "You can go," I say, though I ache at the thought of not being able to see him every day.

Keller reaches over and takes my hand in his. "We will, when you and Egan can go, too."

"The plot thickens," Egan says as he stares at his ever-present laptop. "Our mystery witch responded to a message I posted. Says she's for real, and that she knows of at least two other people who want to leave the covens, too."

"What's your read on her?" I ask.

"Hard to say from an online message, but it's worth exploring more," he says.

I nod. "But explore carefully." I get the craziest image of two witch armies squaring off across a battlefield, good versus evil.

Rule texts us from his last class of the day, telling us he's dying of boredom and to meet him at the shop after school.

"Poor guy," Egan says. "Too bad he's not a delinquent like the rest of us."

Instead of moving the vehicles, we decide to walk to the herb shop. As we're leaving the café, the sound of sirens fills the cold December air. It's not until we're within view of Wiccan Good Herbs that we realize the destination of all those emergency vehicles.

"No!" I say and begin to run. Everyone else follows, but Egan is the only one who can keep up with me.

When I reach the front of the shop, a cop tries to stop me from entering. I don't even think before shoving him hard enough to make him trip and fall backward over a large, terra cotta planter on the sidewalk. I vaguely hear Keller doing damage control, telling the cops that our friends are inside.

I stop in my tracks when I see Rule. His face is pale as death, and I've never seen such raw pain on someone's face who wasn't being siphoned. Next to him, someone has spray painted the front counter. *Evil witches, I will kill you all.*

My heart lodges in my throat as I only vaguely hear one of the police officers say something about a crazy nut.

I push myself past all the hands trying to stop me from getting to Rule. My heart hammers against my ribs, and I'm sick with fear.

I reach Rule. "What happened?" He doesn't speak, doesn't even seem to hear me. I shake him. "Rule, what happened?"

He looks past me, and I follow the path of his gaze. Fiona lies behind the front counter, a hole in her chest and a pool of blood on the floor below her. For a moment, I think I might faint. But then a scream claws its way out of me. "No!" I try to push my way to her, but this time it's Keller who grabs me and forces me into the back room, away from the sight of Fiona's body.

My vision changes, and I know my eyes have gone black. The hair all over my body stands on end, and papers blow around the room.

"Stop it," Keller tells me in an urgent whisper. "Not here, not now."

"Yes, now." My voice sounds more like the evil inside me, deeper, animalistic. I feel like an animal. I want to rip the flesh from whoever did this, make them watch as I burn it before their eyes.

It's Adele's sound of anguish from the front of the shop that snaps me back to reality. A torrent of tears and hard, wracking sobs replace the evil, and I collapse against Keller's strong body.

I think back to my conversation with Fiona, how she'd said defeating the covens was worth dying for, that she'd help me in any way she could. But we haven't even faced the covens yet, and I know in the deepest part of me that her killer wasn't a witch. She's dead now because she was protecting me. Amos Barrow killed her for it, probably hoping to draw Egan and me out.

"It's all my fault," I cry.

"Shh, don't say that," Keller says as he holds me close. "It's not true. Shh, it's not true."

I know part of what he's doing is comforting me, but I also sense that he doesn't want the cops asking us questions we can't answer. Like why I would say the murder of a sweet old lady is my fault. I swallow all the pain, all the self-loathing. It will rise to the surface again, but first I have to get away from my friends.

I'm not able to for more than an hour. After the cops question all of us and Fiona's . . . body is taken away, I race out the back door to the alley behind the shop. My breath comes in fast, ragged gasps, and I fist my hands as I lean against the concrete wall. "Where are you?" I scream. "Come out and fight me, you bastard!"

Keller hurries out the door. "What are you doing?"

"Leave me alone, Keller." I move to walk away, but he makes the mistake of grabbing my arm. I fling him away, and part of me isn't even sorry. Instead of taking a hint, he comes for me again. I hold up my fingers to let him see the electricity arcing between them.

"You won't use that on me," he says.

"Won't I? I'm a dark witch, remember? I bring destruction

wherever I go."

"Stop it!" He stares hard at me. He jabs his finger toward the back door. "There are people hurting in there, so this is no time for self-pity."

I use my witch speed to cross the distance between us faster than he can see. I get right in his face. "Who do you think is responsible for those sad people?"

"Amos Barrow," he says, not cowed by me in the least.

"And he would not be here, would not even know who Fiona is . . ." I choke. "*Was* if it weren't for me."

Keller grips my shoulders. "She knew the dangers." His voice breaks, and his own sorrow sobers me, makes me really listen to his words. "We all do, and we stand by you anyway. Because we believe in you, Jax. We believe in you and your goal of ending the coven threat."

Fresh tears track down my cheeks. "But I can't even save you from a human. What am I supposed to do when covens of dark witches come at us?"

He lifts one of his hands and cups my jaw. "What you have to. You've already saved us once at Shiprock, and I don't have an ounce of doubt that you'll find a way to do so again."

"But Fiona . . ."

"You weren't here, Jax. You can't save someone if you're not even here."

"I shouldn't have left her alone."

"How were you supposed to know Barrow would go for her?"

"I just should have." I start crying hard again, and Keller pulls me tight against him. After a couple of moments, I hear him sniff, and I know that he is crying, too. In such a short time, Fiona had become like family, a grandmother to love and be loved by. And now she's gone, gone forever.

My grief gives way to anger, and I flee from the herb shop. I run up one street and down another, hoping Amos Barrow will find me. When all I get is some curious looks from the area residents, I race to Sarah's house, using my superhuman speed and not caring if it attracts the covens. Let them come. Let them all come. I'll take on them all, and I'll destroy them.

I'll make Sarah give me whatever information she's been holding back. I'll force her to tell me how to access all of my white witch power so I can end the covens' tyranny for good.

So I can make Amos Barrow pay for what he did.

When I stop in front of Sarah's house only to find she's not there, the darkness inside me roars to life. I reach out with my senses to find Sarah or anyone else with a similar signature. When I don't sense anything, I increase the flow of magic.

"Where are you?" I yell, not caring if the neighbors think I'm crazy. Maybe I am.

Keller's truck screeches to a halt at the curb. He, Toni and Egan hop out and head straight for me. I stare hard at them, not wanting them here.

"Jax, what are you doing?" Keller asks as he draws near.

"What I should have done long before now."

"Bring every damn coven down on our heads before we're ready?" Egan asks. "Cut the power surge, will ya?"

Keller tries to take my hand, but I back away. "No. I'm going to find the Bane, and they are going to tell me how to gain enough power to end this."

"You're hurting. We all are. But we have to think things through."

"I'm tired of thinking things through! I'm tired of waiting. I'm tired of worrying about someone getting hurt. None of it does any good."

Toni steps forward. "Jax—"

Egan moves fast and grabs my upper arm. "Stop it, right now, before you get us all killed! Unless that's what you want."

I've never seen Egan look so fierce, so angry, so . . . adult and in charge. It's enough to shake some sense into me. What *am* I doing? I cut the flow of my power, wondering if I've truly lost my mind. Hoping I haven't let the darkness inside me sign our death warrants.

Chapter Twelve

When night falls, we all sit around the old dining room table in the farmhouse's kitchen watching as Keller talks to his father on the phone. When he finally ends the call and turns toward us, he's holding a sheet of paper.

"Barrow's contact number," he says.

It feels wrong to still assume the leader's position after what I did earlier, putting us all at even more risk than we were already in, but it's my responsibility. I put us in this mess, and I'll get us out.

"The old Pherson property," I say. "I'll set up a meeting there. The line of trees will provide cover. I will draw him out, and you two," I say, pointing at Egan and Keller, "will come around him from behind. Toni, you will be armed and guarding the perimeter, letting us know if anyone else approaches."

"What about me?" Rule asks. He hasn't said much since he and Adele arrived at the farm, unable to stay in their home tonight, not when Barrow could come back.

"You stay here with your mom."

"No," Adele says. She's slipped out of the bedroom where she was resting. Her eyes are red and puffy, but there is a resolve in them that I recognize as her mother's. "This man killed my mother. I'm not going to sit idly by and do nothing while I send children off to fight him. I know you're all stronger than I am, but I can't do nothing."

I nod, understanding her need to take action. "You two can help Toni guard the perimeter. That will give us more coverage in case Barrow has alerted other hunters or witches start showing up."

Once we have all the plans in place, I take out my phone and with shaky hands text Barrow's number. When I hit the send button, I place the phone on the table in front of me and stare at it. "Well, that's that."

We all sit in silence for several seconds before I make eye contact with Keller. "I need you to remember what you promised me."

Keller takes a deep breath and looks away. "It won't come to that."

"You saw me earlier. You know it might."

"What is she talking about?" Toni asks, looking anxious at the tone of the conversation.

"He promised that if I went totally over to the dark side and was in danger of hurting someone, he would kill me."

"Kill her?" Toni nearly shrieks her disbelief. "And you promised this?"

"It's only as a last resort," he says.

Toni shoots up from her chair and paces across the room, her palm pressed against her forehead. "Oh, my God. I can't believe I'm hearing this."

Egan meets my eyes and holds them for a long time. "We need you to keep fighting the darkness. I need you." He lets that sink in for a moment. "Barrow's a piece of garbage, but we can take care of him without you caving."

I nod. "Let's get everything ready."

When everyone stands and starts gathering coats, Egan pulls me aside. "I know it's hard, but you have to keep fighting it," he says so no one else can hear. "I'm afraid if you give in, I won't be far behind."

It's the first time he's actually admitted out loud to being afraid of anything. More than anything else that's been said, his words help beat back the rising darkness. I realize how much I care about him. He's like the brother I've never had.

We work side by side loading weapons and flashlights into the Jeep and truck. Our feet make a muffled crunching sound as we walk through a layer of newly fallen snow. The land as far as I can see is wearing a blanket of white. It really is beautiful in a lonely, frigid way.

"If we find a way to defeat the covens, are you going back to Baker Gap?" Egan asks.

I shake my head slowly. "I can't think that far ahead. It takes more energy than I have at my disposal."

"Because I am. And after Toni graduates, I'm going to go wherever she wants to for as long as she'll have me."

It feels foreign, like a language I once knew but have forgotten, but I smile. "Head over heels, huh?"

"Yep."

"Never thought I'd see the day, but I'm glad." I point at him. "You treat her right, or you'll have to deal with me."

He just smiles, but I can tell by the emotions filling him to the brim that his parade of arm candy is over. Despite what I told him about not looking too far into the future, I allow myself to imagine a time when the covens are no longer a threat and I'm free to be who I want to be. Free to be with Keller and over-the-moon happy. I try not to let myself think about how tiny a chance there is of that happening.

My phone buzzes in my pocket, a text coming through. When I see the message, the darkness surges upward like a tidal wave, flooding me with the potent desire for revenge.

"What does it say?" Egan asks.

"Barrow's changing the game plan." I read the text to everyone. "One hour, Wildwood Cemetery. Come prepared to die."

"We can insist on him coming to us," Rule says.

I shake my head. "He won't show. We go now, or we won't know where or when he might strike. I don't want him to be a threat to you anymore."

We don't drive all the way to the cemetery. Instead, we park the Jeep and Keller's truck in the dark shadows next to an out-of-business convenience store. After assigning Adele and Rule to stand guard at the end of the lane that leads to the cemetery and to call if they see anything off, the rest of us walk toward the cemetery. We keep to the deeper shadows at the edges of the road. Our approach reminds me of when Egan and I headed for Shiprock to face my coven. I'm a much different witch now. I know the kind of damage I can do, and I'm burning with a need to avenge Fiona's death.

I scan the night for threats. But all I see are the dark shapes of trees amongst the falling snow. Flakes land on my nose and cheeks and melt, making my face even colder. Everything around us is still and quiet, too much so. We make it all the way to the cemetery, but I still don't sense Barrow. He's probably the type of guy who likes to put his prey on edge, make them wait until their nerves frazzle. Well, I'm not his normal prey.

I sense Barrow's presence a moment before I hear the approach of a bullet. "Get down!"

Using my fastest speed, I jump out of its path as I push Keller to safety. Shards of stone fly when the bullet hits a gravestone behind me. I send a surge of my power in his direction, but I miss him. Instead, I de-bark half of a tree.

"Come out, you evil bastard!" At the memory of Fiona's crumpled body on the floor, the darkness within me rushes to the surface, but I force it back down. I will not give in.

"I am not the evil one," he says then takes another shot.

I avoid it and send another blast his way. I can't see him yet, but I can sense where he is.

"Keep him talking," Keller whispers and slips off into the night.

My heart constricts in fear. Then I realize the best way to keep him safe is to divert Barrow's attention and let Keller do what he's trained to do.

"I haven't killed an innocent old woman," I spit at Barrow.

"She was far from innocent. She was a witch. Not as black-hearted as you and your kind, but an unnatural being nonetheless."

My magic crackles like lightning along my arms and dances at my fingertips. My body shakes with the effort to keep it in check. "Who are you to decide who is evil and who isn't? You're obviously not very good at it." I send another bolt his way, staying clear of Keller and causing snow from the ground to shoot into the air.

"There is no place in this world for evil beings, and some of us have answered the call to purge the world." He sounds like a religious zealot, one so far gone that he can't see that there wasn't an evil bone in Fiona's body. He's no different than the people who started the covens' reign of evil by persecuting innocents during the witch trials.

"You're worse than half the things you hunt," I yell back at Barrow.

"Says a witch so filled with poison that her eyes are black with it, that her body sizzles with the power of Satan."

I make a subtle motion for Toni to stay hidden but watch my back before I walk forward. I stalk through the snow toward his voice, sending blasts of power toward him. I'm not trying to kill him, just keep his attention on me until Keller and Egan can converge and capture him. For a moment, I imagine forcing the life from him, watching his face when the light goes out, the way he watched as Fiona's dimmed then died. It's so difficult to pull myself from those evil thoughts. I know hate fuels the darkness, but I can't help it. I hate Amos Barrow with every fiber of my being.

The momentary lapse of concentration on my part is all Barrow needs. He walks out of the trees, and he has his gun pressed to Rule's temple, a gag in Rule's mouth and his hands bound behind him.

My heart starts beating frantically. How did Rule get here? Where is Adele? Is she still alive? Have I failed their family all over again? "Let him go."

"No."

"I could kill you where you stand," I say with slow, deliberate words.

"Before I pull the trigger and litter the snow with his brains?"

I growl, and the dark magic within me roars to the surface.

"Fight it, Jax," Keller says from somewhere off to my right.

Barrow doesn't even flinch. He's known where Keller and Egan are all along. "She can't," he says, sounding supremely confident and pompous. "It's who she is. Evil. An abomination."

"Shut up!" My voice doesn't sound like my own, and it doesn't even scare me. Some part of me whispers to keep fighting the darkness, but it's so much easier not to, to do what it wants. What I want.

"Take the two of us," Egan says. "Just let the others go."

"He won't let any of us go," I say. "He plans to kill us all." Images of Fiona in that pool of blood assault me. And now the man who killed her holds the life of her grandson in his hands. Rule—my friend, the boy I'd promised to protect to the best of my abilities. I flex my fingers and walk slowly forward, stalking my prey. "Only he's the one not leaving."

"Jax," Toni says behind me, but I ignore her.

"That's it," Barrow says. "You're the one I really want."

When he presses the barrel of the gun harder against the side of Rule's head, I sense Rule's fear, see it in his eyes. It throws gasoline on the fire of my anger, and I catch Barrow unaware as I invade his mind.

He winces with what must feel like a sudden headache. "What are you doing?"

I sift my way through the layers of his mind until I find the right spot, and in the next instant he releases Rule. Keller races out of hiding to get Rule, who has fallen to his knees and is having difficulty getting back up.

Barrow fights back unexpectedly. "Get out of my brain!" He raises the gun.

I don't give him any time to aim at Rule or Keller. I send a blast of magic into him that is so powerful he goes airborne before falling on his back into the snow.

Hatred churns inside me, and I let more of the darkness take over as I blast him against. This time, it makes his coat smoke.

Egan tries to run for me, but I use my greater power to toss him aside before he reaches me.

"Jax, stop it!"

I turn and see Keller aiming a gun at me from the lane.

"Keller, no," Toni says.

Egan pulls himself to his feet, and I can tell he is struggling with his own inherent darkness coupled with my increased darkness pulsing through the connection between us. Still, there's enough goodness in him that he crosses to Toni in time to keep her from approaching me.

"Jax, please stop," Toni yells at me. "Please don't make Keller do this."

I can't see them, but I know tears are streaking down her cheeks. Part of me is sorry about that, but a bigger part doesn't care. I'm still self-aware enough to know that is not a good sign, that I'm losing the battle for myself.

"Shoot her," Barrow says from where he's managed to prop his battered body on one arm.

I spin back toward him and extend my hands.

"Jax. Jax, look at me." Keller walks closer, his boots crunching in the snow.

Ignore him. He's nothing. I'm tempted to obey the voice of the dark, but a sliver of the girl who loves Keller shifts my attention back to him. *He's a hunter, too. Kill him. Kill them both.*

"I don't want to do this." Keller's voice is strained as he eyes me down the barrel of his shotgun. I know it's not loaded with rock salt this time. I imagine I see the glint of tears in his eyes.

I stare at him, saying nothing, as the darkness rages inside me. The energy pulsing inside me increases each moment, like a power plant about to overload.

"You're a disgrace," Barrow says through his pain. He's not talking about me. The disgust in his voice is for Keller, who is hesitating to do what Barrow has already tried.

"Shut up," I say when I turn my attention back to Barrow. "I'm sick of your voice." My own voice deepens, the darkness speaking.

"Then I hope you hear it for eternity as you burn in hell. You'll burn right alongside all your friends." He lifts the gun he's managed to retrieve while I wasn't looking.

Knowing I can dodge the bullets, I give him a few little shocks, prolonging his agony. He grips the gun as if it's glued to his hand.

"Jax, that's enough." Keller's voice barely makes it past the screaming darkness.

I glance back at him for only a moment, but it's long enough for Barrow to aim his gun. Only he's not aiming at me. His sights are trained on Keller. He pulls the trigger at the same time as I hit him with the full force of my power. I shriek as my power lifts me off the ground, makes my hair fly wildly in all directions. Darkness blackens everything around me, even the pure white of the snow, as I drift toward Barrow's body crumpled on the ground. He has to be dead now, but I don't let up my barrage.

As I stare down at him, my power goes out like a blown bulb, and I fall to the ground. My mind slows, slogs through every thought as if my synapses are caked in molasses. I'm vaguely aware of a pain in the back of my neck, but I can't lift my arm to examine why. My sight blurs at the edges, but I blink enough that I realize I'm lying on my side in the snow facing Barrow. His corpse is smoking and burned beyond recognition. I think I hear someone call out my name, but then my hearing shuts down.

Suddenly, something cold and metallic clamps over my left wrist. Then the worst burning sensation imaginable makes me scream and bow backward. It feels as if my skin is melting, like I've shoved my arm into an open flame. Maybe Barrow was right about me burning in hell. Maybe I'm already there.

Tears leak out of my eyes and drip into the snow. The darkness inside me screams even louder than I do and shrinks away into nothingness. That's when I really see Barrow and realize what I've done. My stomach churns at the horrific image. I did this. I killed a man. Oh my God, I've lost the battle. I wonder about my friends as my vision begins to fade. Movement around me makes me look up, past what is left of Amos Barrow. Red-cloaked figures, ones without faces, stare down at me. I am in hell, and the devil has come to greet me personally.

Coming Soon

MAGICK (Book 3 of the Coven Series)

September, 2012

Read on for an excerpt

MAGICK

(Excerpt)

by Trish Milburn

I wake not to flames but a windowless stone room. For an addled moment, I think I'm in the basement of the herb shop. A stab of pain hits me in the heart, and tears pool in my eyes. Fiona, the woman who'd found her way into my heart as a sort of surrogate grandmother, is gone. Dead. Killed by the man who should have killed me instead. I blink against the tears and look at my surroundings. The bare room isn't the hidden repository of witchlore below Wiccan Good Herbs. It's also not the cold, snow-covered ground where I lost consciousness.

Where I killed Amos Barrow. Where I gave in to the darkness inside me. After fighting so hard against it, Barrow shot his gun at Keller, the boy I love, and I lost my last shred of control.

Fear shoots through me, stealing my breath. Keller. God, is he even alive? Did Barrow take everything from me? The urge to kill him all over again wells up inside me, followed quickly by nausea.

My stomach churns and I turn to the side to retch. When I'm finished, I can't even lift my hand to wipe my mouth. I'm chained to a big, thick chair that reminds me of a medieval throne. My feet are as immovable as my hands, and panic surges to the surface. I try to draw on my power, but it's not there.

Oh, God, what has happened to me? Where am I? Another image settles into my memory, one of red-cloaked figures surrounding me just before I lost consciousness. The Bane. Had Sarah played me all along, making me think she was working with me until she and the other members of the Bane had the opportunity to take me out? Did they capture Egan, too? What about Toni, Rule and Adele? I swallow hard again when I think of Keller and wonder if my actions led to his death. I can't live with that. Losing him, losing my friends would be so much worse than losing myself.

I fist my hands in anger and frustration, instinctively trying to draw on my magic. But there's nothing, not the least inkling of power. I scan my surroundings again, panic swelling more with each breath. Is it possible the Bane stripped me of my power? Is there a way to do so without using a Siphoning Circle? Is that what the burning in my arm was after I slumped to the ground to face Barrow's corpse?

I look at my lower arm but can't see the damage because it's covered with my long-sleeved T-shirt. But it doesn't matter. More than anything, I need to find Keller. I have to believe he's alive. I can't even think otherwise. I yank against the manacles holding my wrists and ankles to thick metal rings. I pull so hard that sweat beads on my forehead and my joints ache with the effort, but it's no use. I'm helpless, at the mercy of whoever walks through the door across from me.

The tears finally spill over and track down my cheeks. Not knowing Keller's fate is killing me.

But do I deserve to know after what I did? Do I even deserve to survive when I killed a man? Yes, he'd been vile, a murderer, but that didn't give me the right to take his life. But I had, and I still remember the horrible sense of glee I'd felt rushing through me as I did it. When I gave in to that writhing darkness that had been itching to consume me since I drew it from the earth, I'd done much more than kill a man. I'd ceased to care that using that level of magic would endanger my friends, would bring the covens to Salem in all their awful fury.

I swallow against the surge of bile. If the covens haven't already arrived, they will soon. And I have no confidence I can save my friends from the vindictive evil of my family, of Egan's,

of all the other dark covens. I am nothing more than a complete and utter failure.

I lean my head against the high back of the chair and stare at the ceiling. I try not to hyperventilate as I replay the events of . . . whenever that was that I killed Barrow. I feel hollow and raw inside, like someone has scooped out anything that had ever been good about me.

Once I get my breathing under control, I check the room again, desperate for some means of escape. I have to get out of here, find my friends, make sure they're safe. I'll take whatever punishment I must, but I have to find them first.

But there are no windows, no other furnishings, nothing on the walls. I have no sense of how long I've been here, have no idea if it's day or night. The minutes stretch, but nothing changes.

"Hello? Can anyone hear me?"

No one answers, and I worry that maybe this is all in my mind as I'm dying. Maybe I am still on the ground, moments away from death. Did Keller actually kill me as I asked him to, and the red-cloaked figures were just a hallucination brought about by my imminent death? I shake my head. That doesn't seem right. I remember a stinging prick in my neck followed quickly by fire racing along my veins. Poison? So I'm lying in the snow with poison burning the life out of me. Maybe it's a fitting way to go for a killer like myself.

A couple more minutes tick by, and the fog surrounding what happened lifts a little. I consider that I'm not dead, but I've instead gone stark-raving crazy. I'm drifting through thoughts I don't want to have when the door suddenly opens. At first, no one comes in, no one is even visible. I'm still out of it enough to think that I've imagined it. I know I didn't open the door because I'm currently as powerless as Toni and Keller.

I'm beginning to think it's one of the spirits Keller and his father hunt when someone appears in the doorway and starts walking toward me. I blink several times, trying to focus. As the woman draws close, I recognize her. Sarah Davenport.

Anger explodes out of me, surging against my restraints

until they catch me. "You! You did this to me."

"Yes." Nothing more. No apology, no explanation, nothing.

"You betrayed us. Where the hell were you? We needed help!"

"No, you are the betrayer." Her words hit me like a punch to the gut because I know she's right. "Because of you, the covens will return to Salem. And when they do, more people will surely die."

Author Biography

The first book Trish Milburn ever wrote was a romance. She just didn't know it yet. That book, *Land of the Misty Gems*, was a class project way back in the sixth grade. She wrote the text, illustrated the book with colored pencils, even bound it with twine and pasted a fabric cover on her creation. And now—mumble-mumble years later—she still has that book. It was the beginning of her writing career, even if until the early 1990s that writing consisted mainly of research papers and essay test questions and then newspaper articles.

Trish was born and grew up in Western Kentucky and began reading so long ago she doesn't really remember how it all started. She does remember loving a little book called *The Runaway Pancake*, then the regular treasures that would appear in her mailbox from the Weekly Reader Book Club, then books like the Little House on the Prairie series. The library was one of her favorite places. And even though being a bookworm didn't do wonders for her social life when she was in her teens, she wouldn't trade her love of books for the world.

After college, she worked as a newspaper reporter and magazine editor and still does some freelance writing and copy editing. But most of her writing now is fiction, and no matter what kind of story it is she can't resist putting at least some romance in it alongside the paranormal or suspense elements. Her writing has finaled in Romance Writers of America's Golden Heart Contest eight times, winning twice. *White Witch*, her February 2012 release from Bell Bridge Books, was the 2007 Golden Heart winner in the Young Adult category.

In her free time, she loves watching movies and TV (she bought herself a TiVo when she made her first sale), hiking, reading and road trips.

Lightning Source UK Ltd.
Milton Keynes UK
UKOW03f0629100217

294015UK00002B/46/P